MR. HOT HALLOWEEN

A Spicy Holiday Romance with Heart
From One Halloween Night to Christmas Forever

Kandie Kissimmie

Dedication

For everyone who's ever wished:
"What if the Hallmark movie had spice...
and the hero wore a mask?"

From jack-o'-lanterns to twinkle lights,
love doesn't keep a calendar.

Contents

1. Masks & Mischief   1

2. Capes & Carseats   9

3. Doorways & Nerve   17

4. Exits & Orbit   23

5. Clues & Candlelight   31

6. Balcony & Belonging   43

7. Rhythm & Risk   55

8. Keys & Consent   69

9. Notes & Noise   83

10. Glitches & Grit   93

11. Late & Certain   101

12. Thresholds & Recognition   109

13. Catch & Crack   113

14. Shock & Steady   117

15. Knots & Confession   125

16. Lists & Presence   131

17. Flame & Food   135

18. Lights & Letters   145

19. Proof & Pulse   159

20. Cider & Intent   163

21. Lace & Limits   167

22. Patterns & Peace   175

23. Gumdrops & Guilt   179

24. Cinnamon & Certainty   185

25. Ribbon & Relief   189

26. Boxes & Beginnings   193

27. Systems & Shifts   199

28. Frost & Forever   203

29. Storm & Steering   207

30. Dawn & Delilah   213

31. Rockers & Roots   217

Epilogue: Masks & Forever   223

About the Author   231

What You're Getting Into

pairing:

Scarlett × Eli (age gap; older single dad; anxious-artist × steady protector; masquerade meet-cute)

setting:

Crescent Hotel Halloween ball → family holidays (October through Christmas) → a few months later

tone:

high-heat, high-heart; cozy, protective, emotionally steady with soft-dominance and found-family warmth

kinks & tropes:

age gap · single dad · masked ball/secret identities · wrong-name mix-up · one-night-stand → more · fated-feel reconnection · surprise pregnancy (wanted) · gentle dominance/competence kink · praise kink · "you're safe with me" protective hero · found family

· holiday romance (Halloween → Christmas) · proposal epilogue

he says it like he means it:

- "Tell me to stop." — "I've got you."

- "You're not alone in this."

- "Next time? I'm not stopping at a kiss."

- "Stay. This time, stay."

content warnings:

explicit sexual content; on-page surprise pregnancy, prenatal visits, and labor/birth; brief anxiety/panic; alcohol (champagne) and mild profanity; age/experience difference with no workplace/authority dynamic; enthusiastic consent throughout; no cheating; HEA.

Prefer closed-door? On-page intimacy appears in Chapters 7, 8, and 21; you can skim and still enjoy the full story.

CHAPTER 1
Masks & Mischief

One night. One risk. One man you shouldn't want.

SCARLETT

Some spend Halloween in sequins and glitter. I spend it in leggings, drowning in a couch that could swallow a small car, pretending a single pumpkin counts as festive décor. Tessa calls me a Halloween Scrooge, but honestly, a blanket and tea sound better than elbowing through crowds in heels.

Down the hall, she's been humming for the past hour. Normally it's bubbly, contagious—the kind of sound that makes me want to peek in and compliment her eyeliner. Tonight it keeps slipping sharp, like her breath can't catch up. The longer it goes, the more my eyes snag on the same line of my book. I tell myself she's just excited, but the pitch scrapes like something forced.

Then her voice cuts sharp and wrong.

"Scarlett!"

I'm already half rising when she stumbles into the doorway—mask dangling from her fingers, one hand pressed to her stomach, the other braced against the frame. Fever has her cheeks blotched red, eyes glassy.

"Oh my god, Tess." My book hits the table as I dart under her arm. Heat rolls off her, shocking against my palm. "Sit."

She tries to smile, then winces. "Maybe it was something I ate?"

She's trying to downplay it, but her legs are shaking.

"It's probably nothing. I just need to lie down for a bit."

"Are you serious? You're about to keel over." I guide her to the couch, heart beating too fast. "We'll figure the party out after you breathe."

"But I've been looking forward to this for weeks," she protests, words slurring at the edges. "Do you know how hard it was to get a ticket? Crescent Hotel. Party of the year."

"I know." I tuck the blanket around her legs—the one she teased me for always hoarding. "You're the Halloween queen. But are you sure you should go? You don't look so great."

"Oh, stop being such a Scrooge." She tries to tease but it lands flat. "You're perfectly happy staying in—reading, handing out candy to trick-or-treaters that won't even show."

"That's the dream," I murmur, brushing hair from her damp forehead.

Her laugh snaps into a grimace. Color drains out of her face.

"Tessa, you're burning up." I press my hand to her forehead—hot, dry. Panic pricks behind my ribs. I grab a glass from the kitchen, fill it with water, and kneel beside her. "Sip slow," I remind her, because she always gulps to prove she's fine.

"It's just a bug," she mutters. "I'll be fine in a bit."

She's not just sick; she's grieving the night she built in her head.

"I'm calling it—bed." I try to soften it. "I've got you. We can put on a movie. Rom-com or haunted one you'll regret later?"

"The costume... the makeup..." Her shoulders sag. Defeat drops her voice. "I've been waiting all month for tonight."

"I know it sucks." I squeeze her hand. "But your health wins. The party can wait."

She swallows, then looks at me with fever-bright eyes. "I need you to do something for me."

"Anything."

"You have to go for me," she whispers.

I blink. "What? Tess, you need rest. We'll both stay in—"

"No." Her headshake is too hard, makes her dizzy. "If I can't go, at least you should. Tell me everything tomorrow. I'll live vicariously through you."

I falter. "I can't. I don't even have a costume."

"Yes, you do," she says, firm despite how pale she's gone. "We're the same size. The Catwoman one is all laid out on my bed. It'll fit you. No one will even recognize you, Scar. Come on—do this for me?"

My chest tightens. Parties are not me. Wearing *that* costume—definitely not me. And I can't just leave her here alone. No feels cruel. Yes feels like stepping naked into a crowd.

"I don't know. I'd look ridiculous."

"You wouldn't." A ghost of a grin. "You'll look amazing."

I chew my lip. The idea tilts my stomach. But her pleading hope is impossible to refuse.

"You'll meet people," she adds, throwing spaghetti at the wall. "Have some fun. Maybe even meet a guy. Scar, it's been two years since Eric. You deserve a little fun."

"Maybe. But what if it's just... the same?" The words slip before I cage them. "All the guys I've dated have been so immature. I try to talk soul-deep and they skim the surface. Boys."

Her eyes spark despite the fever. "Then maybe you need someone older. Grounded. You've always been an old soul. You need someone on your level."

"Oh, so now you're my matchmaker?" I try for dry, land closer to fond.

"Stranger things have happened on Halloween." A shaky smile. "Who knows? Maybe tonight you'll meet someone who gets you."

The words land heavy. I've almost stopped believing in that—being understood.

"I don't know, Tess. I'm not sure I'm ready."

"You're ready." Conviction slices through her weakness. "Just go, have fun, be someone else for a night. What's the worst that could happen?"

I blow out a breath and feel myself tip. "Okay. I'll go. But only for a little while." I point at her. "And I'm asking Mrs. Carter to check in on you."

Relief smooths her face. "Thank you, Scar. You're the best. You won't regret it."

Her room is chaos—clothes, palettes, accessories exploded across every surface. The Catwoman costume waits on the bed, sleek and unapologetic. Anxiety prickles as I pick it up.

"Come on, you'll look great," she calls weakly. "Just own it. Tonight could be an adventure."

The suit clings as I work it over my hips, tight in ways that make me tug and shift. The neckline plunges lower than I'd ever choose. I press myself down; the suit presses back, molding me. Exposed. Ridiculous. And, unsettlingly, a little powerful.

The mask cups my breath close; the ears catch the lamplight. The woman in the mirror isn't Scarlett in sweaters and careful routines. She looks like she'll drag me out the door herself.

One night. I can do one night.

I grab Tessa's clutch, steal one last glance at the mirror, heart thundering.

"You look amazing," she says from the couch, voice weak but sure. "Have fun. Don't worry about me."

I nod, half hoping she'll call it off. She just musters a fluttering wave.

"Okay, okay," I mutter, mostly to myself. "I'm going."

My pulse doesn't believe me.

The mask clings as I step into the cool Halloween night. I tell myself it's only an hour, only for Tess. But under my skin, something already knows—this night will change me.

CHAPTER 2

Capes & Carseats

Single dad first. Blind date anyway.

ELI

"Hold still, Lily."

She squirms anyway, skirt brushing my knees as I crouch on the rug. The pink princess costume pools at her ankles, ribbon sliding crooked at her waist. I retie the knot until it sits straight, willing it to stay that way.

The tiara's already slipping again, so I set it square, steady enough to hold its place.

"There." My tone is clipped for precision, but it thaws in the second half. "The most beautiful princess in the whole kingdom."

She giggles, spinning to make the skirt flare. "Daddy, I'm gonna get so much candy! Can we go to Mrs. Thompson's first? She gives out the best chocolate."

"Of course." I smile, already picturing Sam giving in to every detour Lily demands. "You tell Aunt Sam exactly where to go, and she'll make it happen."

Her joy radiates like sunlight. I try to match it, but part of me keeps circling tonight's blind date. Connor swears this woman—Kat—will be perfect. He's been relentless. I remind myself: it's just one night. One date. A permission slip to step outside routine.

Even now, it feels wrong to think of myself first. Protecting Lily's innocence is everything. The thought of bringing someone new into her life—someone who might not stay—ties my stomach in knots.

I smooth a hand over her shoulder, steadying her twirl. "Remember, princess. Say thank you at every house. Even if they give you raisins."

"Ew." She scrunches her nose, but nods solemnly. "Okay, Daddy. I'll be polite."

Lily twirls again, tiara tilting, skirt swishing against my jeans. Her laughter bounces through the hallway, bright enough to fill the whole house. For a second, I let myself breathe. She's ready for tonight. I'm not sure I am.

The doorbell rings. She squeals and bolts ahead of me.

I open the door to Sam, Mark, and their boys. Tyler's cape is already dragging; Ben's pirate patch has migrated to his temple.

"Look who's ready to take on the neighborhood!" Sam crouches, beaming at Lily. "Look at you, Princess! Straight out of a fairy tale."

"Thanks, Aunt Sam." Lily dips into a curtsy so dramatic the tiara nearly topples. I catch it before it hits the porch.

Sam grins up at me as she straightens. "Patricia went overboard on caramel apples. We'll stop by Dad's so the kids can eat themselves sick."

There it is—the reminder. Dad's whirlwind elopement. A second family that somehow works.

Sam's gaze shifts back to me, sharper. "And you, big brother... you look tense."

"I'm fine." Automatic. Too fast.

"Uh-huh." She crosses her arms. "Ready for your big date?"

I shrug. "It's just one date." The words feel too thin against the churn in my gut. *What if it goes well? What if it doesn't? What if I've wasted my time?*

"Exactly," Sam says, nudging me. "Just one date. You'll be fine."

Mark claps me on the back. "Don't let him fool you. He's been dreading this all week."

I roll my eyes, but the grin on his face makes it clear he knows he's right.

Sam leans closer, voice low. "Eli, you deserve this. You deserve a life outside being a dad. Tonight's just about fun. No decisions."

I nod, though the truth loops back to Lily. She deserves a father who's whole. Not a shadow.

"Alright," I exhale. "I'll go. But only because you've guilted me into it."

Sam smirks. "That's more like it."

I head inside for my bag. Essentials only—wallet, phone, a change of clothes. The hotel room is a contingency plan: a place to switch, a place to crash if I drink, a controlled variable in a night that already feels unpredictable.

The Zorro costume waits inside. Black pants, black shirt, cape, hat, mask. Simple. Functional. The cape is too much theater, but Lily begged, and I let her win that one.

Before I leave, I kneel in front of her. She throws her arms around my neck, the candy-shampoo scent in her hair a weight that almost makes me call the whole thing off.

"Be good for Aunt Sam and Uncle Mark, alright? I'll be back in the morning."

Her arms tighten. "Do you have to go, Daddy?"

"I do, sweetie." I brush the curls off her forehead. "But you'll have so much fun tonight. Just don't eat too much candy."

She pulls back, thinking hard. "Okay. But when you come back, can we do something fun this weekend?"

"Deal." I press a kiss to her temple. "Anything you want."

Sam catches my eye as I stand. "Go have fun. You've earned it."

She says it like it's easy. For me, it never is.

My phone buzzes. Connor's text glows:

> Good luck tonight, E.J. Kat's in a kitty-cat costume. Meet her by the bar at 8. Meow.

I roll my eyes. Of course he'd add that.

But after the smirk fades, I keep staring at it. He makes it sound simple. I already feel the knots tightening.

As the kids tumble down the porch steps, Sam glances back. "You know, Dad's elopement with Patricia was crazy, but it works. She's exactly what he needed after all those years alone."

"Yeah. It was a shock. But they're happy."

"Exactly." Her look is pointed. "Proof you can find happiness when you least expect it. Don't close yourself off."

I hate how she says it like I already am. But she's not wrong. Dad makes it look effortless. It never is. He didn't have Lily in the backseat of his choices.

Still, his life flipped in an instant. Maybe mine could too.

I grab my bag and step into the cool Halloween air. The strap digs into my palm until my knuckles ache.

It's just one night. One chance to test if there's room for more than fatherhood. She deserves a dad who breathes easy. Maybe tonight I'll remember how.

CHAPTER 3

Doorways & Nerve

You almost bolt—then you see him.

SCARLETT

The Crescent Hotel looms ahead, its stone face glowing under a sickle moon. Low mist spills across the stone steps, swirling between costumes as guests drift inside. Laughter, bass, a staged wail—festive, electric. But the current runs around me, not through me.

My stomach knots. Arms cinch tighter across the Catwoman suit, shoulders creeping up. I could turn back—tea, blanket, sketches scattered across the coffee table like armor. No one would know.

Except Tessa.

Her voice echoes—*go, have fun, be someone else for a night.*

I hand over the ticket. A rubber stamp kisses my wrist, the ink stark against my skin. My pulse skips, like it knows this is a one-way door. Fingers flex against the clutch, and I force myself through the opening doors.

Inside, chandeliers drip crystal under gauze webs. Candlelight flickers on marble floors, throwing shadows like the hotel itself is alive, breathing. A skeleton leans in the archway, grinning like it knows my secrets.

Heat prickles under my ribs. My heels click and vanish into the swell of voices, but my stride falters. Arms hug closer, breath shallow. No one's looking, but my brain screams spotlight. Too bright. Too hot.

I miss my mug of tea so sharply it steals my next breath.

The ballroom yawns wide, velvet curtains swallowing the walls, fog skimming ankles. A ghost bride floats past, veil trailing like a sigh. A knight clanks by, his armor absurd and perfect. The workmanship pulls me in for a beat—stitches, spray paint, hours bent over glue guns—and then squeezes. They built this. I'm just wearing it.

Fingers twitch down the seam of the suit at my hip. I keep to the perimeter, searching for a familiar face, but the masks make strangers of everyone.

At the bar, a zombie bartender grins, chocolate "blood" stuck in a tooth. I order something seasonal and forgettable. The first sip burns. Warmth slides down my throat, loosening the knot in my chest. Not courage—I know that. Just something to hold.

I drift to a shadow near the mirror. The glass warps, stretching guests into ghosts. When it catches me, I'm distorted too—thinner, taller, not-me. My stomach flips, chest heavy. My whole body leans toward the exit.

I could leave. Slip out, tell Tess a white lie in the morning, crawl back to safety.

But I hear her hum—the one she makes when she's disappointed and trying not to be. She would have stayed for *me*. I promised I'd try for *her*.

So I tip back the last of the drink. Heat settles low. Arms uncross. Shoulders roll back, chin lifts. Borrowed confidence is still confidence.

My hair falls over one shoulder; the mask presses snug against my cheekbones.

I walk.

Not far—just enough to prove I can. The décor shifts with the light, eerie one second, beautiful the next. Music slows, bass deep and steady, and for a moment the whole room breathes easier.

That's when I see him.

Zorro stands near the dance floor, cape slung easy, mask shadowing his eyes. Confidence rests on him like a second skin—unforced, undeniable. He scans the room, a private smile curving his mouth, as if all this chaos bends toward him.

My pulse jumps. Heat climbs my throat. The suit squeezes tighter, exposing everything.

He looks up. Our eyes lock, brief but sharp, and my breath stutters.

Alive.

The world narrows into a path between us. I hear Tessa again: *stranger things happen on Halloween.*

"Okay," I whisper to my pulse.

And I push off the wall, every step pulling me closer to the man in black.

CHAPTER 4
Exits & Orbit

He maps the room. He chooses her.

ELI

The ballroom swallows sound and throws it back louder—bass shivering through the floor, glass clinking, laughter sparking off crystal. My chest tightens, breath shallow. Jaw clamped, I sweep the room—exits first, then the bar, then the cleanest lanes through the crowd. Once the map's set, I can breathe.

The mask hugs close, warmth gathers at my neck with Connor's text still looping: Cat costume. By the bar. 8. I adjust the edge until it sits flush. Prop and shield. The instructions are simple enough. Run the experiment. My stride angles toward the bar like it's just another variable to control.

Capes and fangs blur past, a knight clanking like he lost a bet with his friends. Then—there. Five minutes to eight, and she cuts through the crush. Black suit, mask, ears—every line deliberate, the cut and finish all intention. Shoulders set before each step, not drifting but choosing motion.

A jolt catches under my ribs. My pulse kicks hard, sharper than I want it to. My stride tightens, carrying me forward before I've even made the choice.

She lifts her gaze just as I break through the last knot of people. Curiosity flickers first, then a softness that lands lower than I expect. My throat tightens; my shoulders square harder, like I'm bracing for impact.

My lips move before I authorize them. "Hey, Kitty Cat." Too easy—lighter than I ever sound. "I'm E.J."

The name fits here. Only family gets Eli. Everyone else gets E.J.—neutral, simple, practiced. A version I can control.

Surprise sparks at her mouth, then tips into a smile. "Nice to meet you, E.J. Or should I say... Zorro?"

Heat loosens down my chest, a notch unclenching. I nod at the sleek lines of her suit—intentional work, not costume-rack filler. "Yours is solid," I tell her.

Her eyes track over mine, a flicker of appraisal without edge. "So is yours." The corner of her mouth curves like it's more truth than courtesy.

The murmur of the room dips, not gone, but muffled under the steadier rhythm in my ears. The tension that rode in with me—Connor's text, the hotel room as backup plan—slides further out of reach. For the first time tonight, standing here feels like a choice I'd make on my own.

I let the silence stretch a breath too long, steadying my pulse, then tip my chin toward her glass. "So what do you do when you're not prowling rooftops as Catwoman?"

She shifts the stem between her fingers, shoulders rolling back like she's setting herself in place. "Graphic designer. Started full-time about a year and a half ago."

A spark catches behind her eyes—new-chapter glow. My chest gives a small pull, an echo from years back. "Good stretch," I say, voice low. "I remember it. Feels like another lifetime."

Her brows lift, curious, testing. "And you? Besides rescuing damsels and fighting injustice?"

The brim of my hat dips under my touch, a reflex to buy space before I answer. My pulse knocks once, heavy, because this is the line that matters. "Programmer," I tell her. My mouth quirks. "Been at it nearly two decades. Which probably makes me the older guy here."

She doesn't miss a beat. Her lips curve, eyes catching the light just right. "Vintage has appeal," she says, teasing threaded with something gentler.

Heat flickers under my collar. My mouth pulls into a dry huff. "I'll take vintage over obsolete."

The DJ drifts into a slowed-down remix, familiar chords bending through the air. *Hey There Delilah*. The file pops open in my head—cramped apartments, cheap beer, the soundtrack to a younger me. My ribs tighten with the years stacked since.

"This was everywhere when I was in college," I say, voice even, as if naming it steadies the math.

Her head tilts, grin tipping sideways. "Not really my era."

Right—confirmation. The gap's real, measurable. My chest stays tight a second longer, then loosens on the exhale. Better to name the variable than let it hover. "Perks of vintage," I say, tone dry. "Comes with stories."

Her eyes spark sharper now, amused and unafraid. "Mm. And experience."

The word hooks low, drags heat through me before I can lock it down. My shoulders square, jaw easing just enough to let the line slip free, unfiltered. "I'm starting to think I like you."

For a heartbeat she pauses, lips parted—not retreating, just processing. Then her smile blooms cleaner, stripped of performance. Something in my chest unwinds, slow but definite, like a knot giving way.

We keep moving, orbiting the edges of the crowd. Conversation flows easy—too easy for strangers. She taps the rim of her glass when she's weighing a thought, angles her body a fraction closer like alignment is reflex, not choice.

The ballroom noise thins to a workable hum. For once, I'm not counting minutes.

Then the math edges back in. She's just starting her runway—mid-twenties, life stretching wide open. I've been measuring in school years for a while now. Every choice hits Lily's orbit. That doesn't disappear because I like the way this woman laughs at my lines.

My stomach tightens with the reminder. My shoulders lock.

But then—no restless scanning past me for shinier options. No performance. Just warmth, ease, attention that lands and stays.

The tension in my chest shifts, loosens. The evidence stacks stubbornly. Connor's pitch was noise. This—her—reads as signal.

I lean a little closer, steady. "Wasn't sure what I'd find tonight. You're a good surprise."

Her smile curves quiet, assent written in her eyes. It hits deeper than it should.

We fall into step, side by side, cutting a clean line through fog and velvet.

Hope pushes in, dangerous as ever. It pulls against my ribs anyway. And for the first time in a long time, I let it.

CHAPTER 5

Clues & Candlelight

Brains first, then a kiss—trust clicks.

SCARLETT

The Crescent hums under my skin now—music thudding through the floorboards, laughter sparking in pockets around the ballroom, a current I can actually feel instead of just watching. My breath quickens, but it isn't nerves this time.

E.J.'s palm rests at the small of my back, light, solid—a touch that steadies and thrills at once. My shoulders ease; before I realize it, I lean into the warmth. I didn't come for this. I came because Tessa asked. Somewhere between the bar and his dry, unhurried smile, I stopped doing it for her and started wanting it for me.

He leans close, his voice slipping through the bass like it belongs there. "Hey, Kitty Cat. Trivia's starting. What do you say?"

Heat flashes up my neck—the nickname should grate, but with him it doesn't. My brow arches; my mouth curves before I can stop it. He looks like he's just discovered treasure.

"Only if we can count TikTok as a category," I say, already smiling.

"Deal." The corner of his mouth lifts, almost smug. "I'll bring the... vintage references."

A laugh bursts from me, easier than it should. "I'm counting on it."

The trivia host is a mad scientist in a foam wig, mic squealing as he tries to corral the crowd. We slide into a table near the front—close enough that I can read the screen and the room, far enough back that it feels like our own small circle carved out of chaos.

The first question drops, and we're off. It's ridiculous how fast we fall into rhythm—answers bouncing between us like we've been playing this game for years. He sweeps through late-'90s pop and obscure computer-nerd curveballs, unflappable. I scoop up the modern stuff, the memes and random internet junk. The table behind us groans every time we edge them out by a second.

E.J. doesn't gloat. He just tips me toward the next one, steady, amused, like he knew all along we had this locked if we wanted it.

The host booms, "What 1980s toy's slogan was 'More than meets the eye'?"

E.J. leans in, eyes sparking like the answer's been waiting for him. "Transformers," he says—not to the room, but to me. "I had the whole fleet."

Laughter bursts out of me, fondness ridiculous and instant—for a man and his plastic robots. "Of course you did. I was a Polly Pocket girl. Maybe a Tamagotchi if I was feeling rebellious."

He tilts his head, conceding with mock gravity. "Then we're evenly matched. Toys, different timelines."

I nudge his knee under the table. "Classic meets current. And vintage is just code for reliable."

His mouth stays straight, but his eyes betray him. "Keep talking like that and I'll get cocky."

By the time the scavenger hunt announcement blares through the mic, our table's littered with victory scribbles and my cheeks ache from grinning. E.J. reads the sign aloud with a look that promises trouble.

"Hidden clues. First team back gets a prize." His brow arches, dry but daring. "Feel like outsmarting the room, Kitten?"

"Obviously." I shove back my chair, buoyant. "Lead the way, Zorro."

The hotel morphs into a playground. We duck behind velvet curtains, paw through side tables, brush dust off our fingers. He works like an engineer—methodical, scanning corners, reading patterns in how the props are arranged. I scan for oddities, the one thing that doesn't belong. More than once, we meet at the same discovery, breathless, grinning, like our brains already know how to dance together.

He squints at the last clue. "A rubber spider." He flicks me a look, one brow raised. "Where would you hide something insultingly obvious?"

"In something nobody wants to touch." I point at a nest of fake webbing.

He reaches in without hesitation. I grab his wrist on instinct. "If it's real, I'm suing."

His mouth twitches. "It's not real. And if it is, I'll take the bite."

It's rubber, of course. He pulls it free, triumphant, and we slap palms like teenagers. The high-five stings, loud and unselfconscious, and somewhere in that sound the rest of the room just... blurs. It's not me against a party anymore. It's us against whatever they throw next.

The haunted maze waits down a corridor lit like a dare, letters dripping red across the sign. I stop at the threshold, eyeing the fog curling out like breath.

"I've never done one of these." My voice comes out lighter than the weight in my chest.

"First time for everything." E.J. offers his hand without ceremony, steady as a post. "I've got you."

I take it. His palm closes around mine, not squeezing, just certain. We step into chill and shadow.

The first jump-scare comes fast—a masked ghoul bursting from a hidden panel—and a scream-laugh rips out of me before I can stop it. My fingers clamp around his forearm, nails biting fabric. He doesn't tease, doesn't flinch, just squeezes back once, firm, steering me through the kink in the path with that same palm at my back.

Doors slam. Fog thickens. Something with a chain hisses from the corner. I cling, swearing between bursts of laughter, insisting I hate him. He just moves forward, unshaken, like this is routine.

When the exit light finally spills over us, I'm doubled over, grinning so hard my cheeks hurt. He looks maddeningly calm, like he could drag me back through five more times just to hear me scream again.

"Cruel," I tell him, breathless.

"Efficient." He deadpans, but the twitch at his mouth ruins the act, and I dissolve again.

The ballroom feels softer after the maze, like the noise has worn itself down. We drift until we find a forgotten corner—candles wavering in brass holders, shadows folding close. It's dim enough that the rest of the party hums like it's behind a wall.

I sink into the quiet, shoulders loosening for the first time all night. E.J. settles beside me, his thigh close enough that I can feel the warmth, steady as a low hum in my skin.

He watches me—not staring, not grazing past. Watching. My pulse skitters, but it doesn't feel invasive. It feels like being held in focus.

"So, Kitty Cat." His voice is low, velvet dragged over stone. "Can I ask you something?"

"Mm." My heartbeat trips again. "Ask."

"How do you feel about kids?"

The question lands heavy, deliberate. Not a joke, not filler. I hold it, turn it over before answering. "I love them. I teach an after-school art class once a week. Mostly little ones. Pure chaos and pure joy." A smile pulls at me, unbidden. "There's this girl, Ella—quiet as a stone, won't look at you, barely speaks. But give her paint and two minutes of silence, and she lights up. Like the light was always there—she just needed someone to notice the cord and pull."

E.J.'s eyes soften, warmth flickering there like it belongs. "That's a gift."

"It feels like one." I tuck hair behind my ear, pulse snagging when his gaze follows the motion.

"I should tell you." He exhales—no drama, just fact. "I'm a full-time dad. Lily's five. Her mom wasn't in the picture, and then she was gone. I didn't even know until there she was—suddenly everything in my life had a new center of gravity."

No polish. No points scored. Just the shape of a life rerouted around a child. The image unspools in my head—front door, a car seat, a tiny face—and something in me goes tender and fierce at once.

"She's lucky," I say. The words scrape rawer than I meant them to.

He dips his gaze, the flicker of a nod like my words weigh more than he planned. "Thanks."

Silence settles, comfortable and alive. The candle beside us throws gold along the edge of his jaw, into the mask's shadow. My skin hums, tuned to the nearness of him—the steady warmth of his thigh, the weight of his attention.

I should tell him my real name. The thought presses sharp against my ribs. I lean in, breath catching, ready.

His mouth tilts. "Yes, Kitty Cat?"

The question lands like an opening. Instead of words, I close the space.

The first brush of his lips is soft, patient. My breath catches, and when I sigh, he deepens the kiss with a certainty that makes my toes curl in my boots. Fingers skim my jaw, the lightest anchor at my waist. Heat spirals through me, low and consuming, and all I can think is *more*.

When we part, the room is blurred at the edges. He stays close, breath ghosting my cheek. His quiet laugh slips out—satisfied but not smug. My chest feels too tight and too open all at once.

We don't move right away. Instead, our voices fall low, spilling into the quiet. Work stories, Halloween candy rankings, his cheat of using patterns for pumpkin carving, my refusal to use stencils because the mess is the point. It doesn't feel like first-date chatter. It feels like dropping into the middle of something we'd already started.

The candle flickers; his profile sharpens and softens with the flame. I tuck my knees toward him without meaning to, pulled by the gravity of ease.

Eventually, the music tugs us back toward the larger room. Bass thuds like a reminder that the world still exists. He threads his fingers through mine as we stand. The contact is ordinary, but it feels anything but—warm, anchoring, like a hinge the whole night swings on.

We walk together, shoulder to shoulder, the noise folding back around us. My chest flutters, caught between giddiness and dread. Because sooner or later, I have to tell him—my real name, the truth I've let slide for too long. And the second I do, the spell changes.

We pass a tall mirror veined with gilt. Our reflection catches—Zorro and his cat, masks intact, a pairing that looks inevitable in glass. My stomach flips. Words hover, ready to spill.

Not yet, I think, coward and honest both. *Before midnight. I'll fix it before midnight.*

His hand squeezes mine, easy, like he heard the thought. "Another drink?"

"Sure," I answer, because right now I don't want to step out of this feeling. Because holding his hand feels like claiming a life I've only ever watched from the edge. And I already know—I can't hold it under a lie forever.

CHAPTER 6
Balcony & Belonging

Step back. Breathe. Go back for her.

ELI

The balcony door shuts with a muffled thump, sealing the bass and chatter into a dull vibration behind me. Cool air cuts sharp across my face, tightening my chest. I roll my shoulders once, palms braced against the iron rail, sting of the chill steadying me. The garden below sits in clean lines, hedges trimmed to symmetry, moonlight sketching every edge in silver. Order. My pulse starts to match its rhythm, slow and exact.

The kiss hasn't left. Heat clings at my jaw, lips pressing together as if her mouth were still there. It's not memory—it's residue, a pull I can't file away. Past relationships ran on clear patterns, manageable, two calendars aligned. This isn't that. This is sharper, stronger, insistent. I log the sensation like I would a new variable, because naming it is the only way to keep it from running wild.

Then the weight comes—the thought of momentum, of letting this move too fast. Breath stutters shallow. My shoulders lock, fingers biting down on the rail until they sting. Lily is baseline. Every decision routes through her first. That filter has kept us safe, predictable. Controlled. I blow out a slow exhale, the night air tearing through my lungs, as if naming the fear will keep it from shadowboxing me.

I drag my focus back to the rail, grounding in the cold bite against my palms. Okay. Facts first. What do I actually know?

She matches me. Trivia—our answers bounced back and forth without jockeying. The scavenger hunt—we spotted the same patterns from different angles and hit the solutions at the same time. The maze—her hand clamped my arm without hesitation, and when I steadied her, she laughed through the fear instead of freezing. And then the corner, the candle-light, the question about kids—she didn't dodge. She met me there, steady, serious.

The image sneaks in before I can shut it down: her in my kitchen, Lily's paint-streaked fingers curled around her wrist, all three of us arguing stencils versus chaos pumpkins. It hits low, dangerous, too easy. My chest aches at the possibility. I cut it off hard, jaw tight. Tempting, but not real. Not yet.

But the thread is strong enough to follow.

I push off the rail before my head builds more futures I can't cash. The door thumps closed behind me and the warmth folds back in—fog, light, motion pressing against my shoulders. I scan the room on instinct. There—by the bar. She's half-turned toward the crowd, head tipped like she's listening under the noise. Then her eyes find mine. Her shoulders shift, just a fraction, and that smile breaks—small, incredulous, like she can't quite believe I'm still here.

A thrum hits low beneath my ribs, pulse pressing heavier against my chest. My focus tightens; everything else in the ballroom dulls to background. She's not drifting—she's looking right at me. Connection reestablished. Clear.

My stride sets without thought, deliberate enough that the crowd slips aside to make room.

I reach the bar just as the couple beside her drifts away, leaving the space open. Heat presses low in my chest, tightening the air in my lungs. My mouth curves before I mean it to, voice slipping out lighter than I feel inside.

"Miss me?"

Her smile edges quick, unguarded. "A little." It doesn't sound like a line.

Her hand settles light on my forearm; her gaze flicks toward the balcony door—a quiet ask. Heat gathers low, clean and electric. My shoulders ease, just enough to register the contact. She left it long enough to mean it. Not accident.

"How's the perimeter?" she asks, mouth tugging.

"Clear." The corner of mine tips in answer. "No ghosts. One moral panic. Resolved."

Her laugh is quick, real, sparking against my chest.

"You always step out when it gets loud?" she asks, eyes glinting.

My breath tightens, a flare of self-consciousness I don't let live long. My gaze slips sideways, then steadies back on her. Better to keep it straight.

"Sometimes," I admit. "I like to make sense of the room before I dive back in." I tip my head, searching her face. "You okay?"

"Better than okay," she says, softer after. "I didn't think I'd be this... in it." Her thumb smooths once over my sleeve before she lets go.

Warmth spreads low, loosening the coil that's been wired there all night. My posture loosens, air moving easier. She's here, in this with me. Not accident. Not noise. Real.

I don't move back. Neither does she. We let the silence hold before the two of us drift along the ballroom's edge, a cadence separate from the crowd.

Her gaze slips toward the dance floor, lights strobing off fog. "So," she says, sly, "does Zorro dance?"

A twist hits low in my gut—half dread, half amusement. My lips press, then tilt despite me; I give a short shake of my head. No reason to fake what I can't sell.

"Badly," I deadpan. "Efficiently."

Her laugh breaks out—quick, unguarded, nothing put on.

Warmth thuds through my chest, pulse dragging deeper. My mouth softens, leaning me closer without thought.

That laugh's the real thing. I want more of it.

I let the corner of my mouth pull, stay in her orbit, and we keep our pace along the edge, the crowd spilling past like weather we don't have to step into.

The talk turns easy—how we moved like a team all night. Trivia, scavenger hunt, even the maze. She gives me a look like it shouldn't have worked, but it did.

I huff, tipping my head. "I've had practice."

She lifts a brow. "With scavenger hunts?"

"With staying calm while someone panics next to me."

Her smile kicks sideways. "Let me guess—Lily?"

I nod, already feeling the memory unspool. "Last spring, she lost her stuffed bunny in the grocery store. Absolute meltdown. Full body sobbing in the cereal aisle."

"No," she whispers, grinning.

"Oh yeah. And the bunny's name is—" I glance over like I'm about to share classified intel. "—Butternut."

She snorts, delighted. "Please tell me you found him."

"Eventually," I say. "But not before we interrogated six employees, checked security footage, and retraced our path like we were in a heist movie. She had me narrating like I was a detective the whole time."

Her laughter spills out—warm and real. It lands somewhere deep.

"When we finally found him wedged behind the granola bars," I add, "she hugged me and said, 'You're good in emergencies. Like a rescue guy. But for bunnies.'"

My shoulders ease just saying it.

She doesn't joke, doesn't deflect—just watches me for a beat, expression soft, like that story told her something important. Something true.

She leans closer, amused. "You make statements like they're neutral facts. Even the ones that aren't."

A pull lands low in my chest—half amusement, half exposure. The corner of my mouth twitches before I let a breath slip out. She's not wrong. Not accusing either. Just naming it.

"Occupational hazard," I say, voice even. "I like understandable systems. Feelings don't always cooperate."

She gestures lightly at the room. "And yet here you are. Masquerade, kissing a stranger in a candlelit corner."

Heat creeps up my collar, my pulse dragging heavier. My shoulders lock, then ease with a small tilt of my head. She's right. But it sounds cleaner my way.

"Running an experiment," I correct, steady.

Her eyes spark. "And your hypothesis?"

A low hum lands under my sternum, pulse tightening with the risk in it. My chest expands on a deeper breath, head tilting as I study her. Honesty costs here, but the cleanest line is the true one.

"That the signal holds if I keep following it," I say. "So far, so good."

The party swirls past us, noise dimmed to background. She studies my face with attention so direct it coils heat steady in my chest, unnerving in its quiet. My jaw works once before I hold still under it. Disarming—she looks at me the way I look at code, like attention is a tool, not a weapon.

"Want to get some air?" I ask, breaking the quiet.

She glances toward the balcony, then back at me. A flicker pulls through my chest—anticipation edged with caution. I keep my shoulders steady, eyes on hers. The step itself matters less than the fact she wants to take it with me.

"Only if you come back in with me," she says.

"That's the plan," I answer.

We step into colder air. She shivers once, quick. A tug pulls low in my chest—protective, warm. I lift the edge of the cape, opening the space between us.

She huffs a laugh, tucks in—like the space was already there. Instinct first, thought second.

The garden lies in its same clean lines, but it reads different with her shoulder resting against my chest. Tension loosens; breath eases until it syncs with hers.

I go still, letting the quiet hold us. No words needed. The silence feels like enough.

Music shifts inside, a new rhythm threading through the noise. She looks up, eyes bright, as if she wants to see what the room has turned into now. The pull tightens low, sharp and insistent. I set my hand on the door, steady. Let her set the pace. What matters is the choice, not the motion.

I hold it open. She goes first.

Noise folds back around us as we step inside. Her hand finds mine, fingers threading through like it's something we've done a thousand times. Warmth spreads low, steady. My grip answers before I think to. An ordinary gesture. A big meaning. I don't let it go.

I used to mistake attraction for fate. Or dismiss it as noise. Neither worked. This isn't prophecy, and it isn't random—it's a string of inputs lining up: the lean-in, the laugh in my chest, the hand that keeps finding me. The risk is high. The reward, higher. Lily's in the backseat of every choice, watching what I do with it.

Hope presses tight against my ribs. My breath stalls, then lets go slow. Shoulders ease. The signal holds.

Strong enough to follow. For the first time in too long, I want to see where it leads.

CHAPTER 7

Rhythm & Risk

The music swells. Your body forgets to be afraid.

SCARLETT

The ballroom thrums too loud—bass through bone, laughter flashing sharp, sequins scattering light until it pricks my eyes. It should press me flat. It usually does. But then his hand finds the small of my back, and the sound tilts off-axis. The blur softens. My ribs feel less like a cage, more like they're remembering how to open. My fingers tighten around his without thought, grateful for the anchor in the storm.

Tessa's voice shadows me—*one hour, Scar. Prove you tried.* I should be watching the door, planning the retreat back to tea and sketches. But his dry smile still lingers in my chest, his palm still warm at my spine. Somewhere in the blur, the night slipped its leash. It isn't just hers anymore. I want it too.

He threads us through the bodies—one clean turn, efficient, not showy. A laugh tears loose—too loud, too naked. My head tips back, hair flying, the suit tugging tight across my thighs. The sound startles me; I almost bite it down. But his palm steadies the turn, and no one's gaze cuts sharp the way I expect.

For once, it doesn't feel like exposure. It feels like light breaking through ribs I've held shut too long. I'm still laughing when the turn slows, breath catching, unwilling to cage it again.

The song softens, bass slowing to something dark and steady. E.J.'s arm tightens, drawing me closer, and the air shifts with it. My breath stumbles, a flutter low and insistent, and before I can catch it I'm leaning into the press of his chest. The party blurs at the edges, noise turned to haze. His gaze pins mine—unblinking, unflinching—and suddenly it feels like the rest of the room is a backdrop built only for this tether.

The way he looks at me... it isn't just a glance, it's a study. Heat pools steady under my skin, loosening something I didn't know I'd locked down. My shoulders drop, my body settling closer without command. He sees me—not just Scarlett who folds into safe corners, but Kitty Cat, bold enough to wear a mask and call it courage. Tonight both halves breathe the same air, and I let his eyes hold me there.

His focus doesn't stray. No restless sweep of the room, no borrowed bravado to keep the mask in place. Just steady, quiet attention that doesn't waver, and the relief of it is sharp enough to ache. My breath lengthens, a shiver threading up my arms. Men my age have always raced to impress, to prove themselves louder, faster. He doesn't have to. The stillness in him steadies me, even as it sparks something hotter beneath my skin. I tighten my grip on his hand, claiming the difference.

The question presses in before I can stop it—what happens when tonight folds back into tomorrow? A pinch twists sharp under my ribs, nerves flutter low. My teeth catch on my lip, my gaze flicking toward the exit like escape would solve it. But my hand stays locked in his, my body anchored in the gravity of him. Fling or regret, I'm not ready to break orbit.

His breath grazes the curve of my ear, low and close enough that the bass seems to ride his voice.

"Do you want to come back to my room with me?"

A ripple runs the length of my spine, sharp and electric, leaving my skin too tight for my body. My pulse stumbles, tripping into a faster rhythm. My breath catches, shallow, like I've stepped into air thinner than it was a second ago.

He must feel it—that pause in my step—because his voice follows, just a little quieter.

"There's a bottle of champagne," he says. "I figured if I made it through the cape, I'd earn something decent to drink. Even if it was solo."

The words land soft, unguarded. Not a move. Just a backup plan—quiet, practical, exactly like him.

I don't do this. I don't follow strangers upstairs. I keep my life measured—books, blankets, routines I can trust. But his hand is still at the small of my back, warm and steady, and the question lingers between us like something alive.

I look at him—really look. Searching for hesitation, for a crack in the calm. But all I see is steadiness, eyes lit with the same quiet spark I've felt all night. No performance. No rush. Just him.

"Yes," I whisper. The word barely clears my throat, but his smile tells me he heard. His fingers close over mine, sure and warm, and the connection is immediate.

We slip out together, the ballroom noise dimming to a muffled throb behind the door. The hall stretches long and hushed, carpet swallowing the echo of our steps. My chest is tight, but not with fear—something heavier, hotter, rising under my ribs with every squeeze of his hand.

It feels like leaving one world for another. Masks and noise fading behind us; shadows and anticipation waiting ahead. My nerves flutter, but the reminder steadies me: Mrs. Carter is with Tessa. Everything is safe. Tonight, for once, I'm free.

The ballroom drops away with a final pulse of bass, the hush of the hall folding over us like a curtain. His hand is still warm in mine, anchoring, but the warmth drifts deeper, low and insistent. My chest flutters, my breath pulling shorter as if my body already knows what's next.

My fingers cling, then ease when he answers with a squeeze. I walk closer without meaning to, thighs brushing, the contact sparking heat that doesn't fade.

The door clicks shut, sealing us into a hush that feels deliberate. The bed is dressed in crisp linen, champagne on ice, the city throwing its glitter against the glass wall. For a beat I stop short, chest tight, pulse kicking hard. My shoulders climb, breath catching shallow. *This looks set—like a scene I don't belong in.*

Then his gaze finds me—steady, warm, the same quiet gentleness threaded through him all night. One hand rises, lifting the hat from his head and setting it aside like he's shedding something heavier. The pinch in my ribs loosens, warmth sliding lower, breath lengthening uneven. Not a prize. Not a performance. Just him.

My heels sink into the carpet. The ballroom is gone. What's left is him.

The cork explodes, sharp as a gunshot. I jolt, heat flashing across my cheeks, and a squeak bursts out before I can stop it. *God, ridiculous.* But the silence breaks, and laughter tumbles out, shaking stiffness loose.

He tilts the bottle with careful precision, foam cresting at the lip, and passes me a glass. The stem chills my fingers; bubbles sting too sharp down my throat. I grip harder, trying to steady myself. *Slow down, Scar.*

He raises his own. "To unexpected nights."

The crystal chime lands sharp, vibrating in my chest. My laugh answers thin, threaded with a pull I can't hide.

We talk—about the maze, the way he never flinched, how I clung like a cartoon koala. About the trivia round where he whispered the answer before the host finished the question.

"Unfair advantage," I tease.

"Vintage wisdom," he counters, deadpan.

I laugh—soft and unguarded, more reaction than choice. Each breath lands easier, the pull in my chest slipping looser. Warmth pools lower. My head tips closer without thinking. Light. Bare. Like I'm not hiding anymore.

Then he steps closer, brushing a lock of hair back. My breath jolts, heat rising too fast beneath my skin. Lips part, but I don't move away. *Stay. Don't retreat.*

"I've got you," he says, low.

My ribs loosen. I set the glass down, palms suddenly free. *Choosing.*

"Tell me to stop," he murmurs, voice steady, rough.

"Don't," I whisper, guiding his hand to the zipper. "I want this."

His mouth finds mine and everything tilts—pulse crashing, stomach swooping, like the floor's been pulled out. A sound spills from me, too soft, too needy—*God*—and still I can't stop. Open, undone. *Yes. Yes.*

The kiss deepens, stubble rasping heat against my skin. I clutch his shirt, chest pressing closer. *More. Closer.*

Still masked, still eared, I climb into his lap, knees sinking into the mattress. Cool air licks my skin where the catsuit slips low, baring my breasts, nipples tightening before his warmth swallows me. Cotton drags rough across them, pulling a gasp against his throat. My back arches, greedy for more.

His thighs spread beneath me, solid, unyielding, grinding me down against him. Pressure sparks sharp with each roll of my hips. Warmth gathers, clings where I need him most. A sound slips out, raw and needy.

His hands steady at my hips, not guiding—just holding. The restraint makes me wilder. My mouth drags down his jaw, open against his throat as my fingers fumble at his buttons, clumsy with urgency. I need him bare.

A groan rumbles low in his chest, the vibration feeding the fire already burning through me. I grind down harder, legs trembling, need breaking through every careful wall.

He catches my wrists, holding firm but not harsh, forcing me to meet his eyes. Hunger darkens them, wicked tilt cutting through my frenzy like a promise. Breath stutters, thighs clamping tighter. If he touches me, I'll splinter.

"I need to taste you," he says, rough, threaded with heat.

The words strike like a spark. Heat detonates low, pressure building sharper. My body arches, offering. *Yes. Take me.*

His grip softens, redirecting—guiding my arms up around his neck as he leans forward, chest to chest, nipples sparking sharp again.

Then he's standing, lifting me as if I weigh nothing. My legs cinch tight around his waist; my breath snags high. He lays me back on the bed in one clean motion, hovering above—careful, certain.

The catsuit gapes open, fabric loose at my waist. Cool air bites damp skin, nerves flaring bright. My thighs twitch together, then yield as his hands steady me apart. Exposed. Offered.

His mouth trails lower—throat, collarbone, breast. Pulse hammers in my chest and belly. I arch hard when his tongue circles a nipple, sucking until a gasp breaks free, slickness gathering deeper beneath the suit.

When he lifts his head, lips slick, eyes dark and clear, my breath holds. "I said I need to taste you," he murmurs. "And I don't mean here."

Heat surges; my thighs fall open without thinking.

He hooks the edges of the suit and peels it down, dragging over hips, then thighs, until it puddles dark at the bed's edge. I'm bare beneath him in the city-lit dark. Cool air shocks, instinct pulling my legs closed. His hands coax them open, patient and steady. *Let him see. Let him have me.*

The first brush of his breath jolts me, hips jerking. My pulse hammers. He doesn't rush, just watches, waiting.

My hips lift, offering.

That's all it takes. His mouth lowers, tongue tracing slow, deliberate. Shock rips through me, tearing a sound loose I didn't know I could make. My back bows off the mattress; his hands lock steady at my hips.

Another stroke, slower, cruel, like he's memorizing me. Heat drags sharp; my thighs snap around his shoulders. He groans, low, the vibration ripping through me, breaking me open. I writhe against him, frantic, breath jagged—*God, don't stop, don't stop.*

The coil inside tightens. I drag him closer by the hair. Take all of me.

Two fingers press inside—stretching, burning, sweet agony—while his mouth seals over me. Shock detonates, white-hot, tearing a cry out of my throat before I can bite it down. My spine arches, everything taut, straining.

He curls deeper, sucks harder, and the coil snaps—violent, shattering. Heat floods out in wave after wave, tearing me apart. I'm gasping, begging—words lost, just sound, just need—as my thighs quake around him, body breaking open, breaking loose.

He doesn't stop—tongue gentling, coaxing me through until I melt, breath scraping raw, chest heaving. Alive everywhere.

When he lifts his head, his mouth glistens, eyes softened with something more than hunger. The look alone sends another shiver down my spine.

I collapse back, trembling so hard the sheets rustle. Breath broken into shards, chest aching. Unraveled. Held steady all at once. Like he tore me apart just to piece me back together.

He trails up my body, kissing stomach, ribs, breast. By the time his mouth meets mine, my chest still heaves too fast, but his kiss steadies it, slow and reverent. The taste of champagne and me mixes dizzy on my tongue.

When he pulls back, his gaze pins me—dark, reverent, desire edged sharp. My pulse jumps.

I shift, and the solid press of him strains hot against my thigh. Heat coils fresh, quick. My palm slides down, brushing him through fabric. His breath roughens, his hand covering mine to guide, pressing me harder.

The reverence is still there, but it rides shotgun to need.

His mouth slows, then stills. My body trembles in shards when he lifts his head. His lips shine, his eyes dark and soft, like I'm something precious in his hands.

The look almost hurts with how much it carries. My throat swallows hard; my chest flutters. *Don't look away.*

I slide shaky fingers through his hair, meaning comfort. His groan vibrates against my palm, reading as invitation. A fresh spark flares in me—*yes, take me.*

He leans in again, kisses lingering, slow and reverent. His mouth is warm, steady, anchoring me back into my own body.

"You're incredible."

CHAPTER 8

Keys & Consent

Ask. Listen. Hold. Stay.

ELI

Her hand slides down, sure and searching, and the second she finds me the world compresses to that single point of contact. Heat arcs through me, brutal in its simplicity. I've been holding the line all night—directing, steadying, controlling. One touch from her and it's gone.

My breath snags rough. I cover her hand with mine, press her harder against me, because restraint feels impossible now. It wasn't enough to watch her unravel—I want to be inside the same storm.

Her eyes meet mine, glassy and wide, not retreating but pulling me with her. And I go.

She's still catching her breath, chest rising fast, cat ears askew. The sight hits harder than it should—not conquest, not ego. Precision. I read her, adjusted, found the edge—and she shattered. That calibration is its own high.

Her lips part like she wants to speak, but what comes is a wrecked little laugh. I answer it with a kiss, slow enough to steady her, deep enough to remind her we're far from done.

Muscle memory takes over—foil, roll, check. One mistake rerouted everything once; I don't leave variables loose. When I push into her, slow and sure, the sound she makes zeroes everything else out. Data I can't ignore: the pace lands, the pressure is right, she's with me. I set rhythm, hips finding the groove where her breath stutters and her fingers dig in.

Her legs wrap high around my waist. I brace one hand under her spine, the other at her hip, controlling angle, depth, drive. Each thrust I adjust by feel, chasing the precise edge that makes her nails bite, her head tip back, her throat spill that broken sound.

"Let go again," I murmur against her jaw, voice low enough to pass for thought.

Her body tightens—signal confirmed. She breaks, loud and unguarded, and I hold steady through it, jaw locked, control burning. *Not yet.*

For a beat, I don't move. I let myself feel the weight of her, the heat, the want still coiled tight under my skin.

I brush her damp hair back, then reach up and ease the mask from her face. "I want to see all of you," I murmur, voice raw with feeling.

Her breath catches. Then she nods.

She reaches up, fingers grazing the edge of my own mask. "You too."

I let her lift it away. The moment holds—quiet, real. No aliases. No costumes. Just us.

Then I ease out, slow and steady, jaw tight against the loss. She shifts beneath me, rolling to her knees, palms braced flat, back arched in open invitation.

For a beat I just take her in—the same woman who edged careful along the ballroom wall now giving me this without hesitation. Trust did that. Trust I won't waste.

I steady her waist, draw her back to me, and push in again. The heat of her makes me groan before I can clamp it down. She gasps—sharp, honest—and the sound strips me raw. Deeper lands; steadiness keeps her with me.

The headboard catches rhythm, thudding in counterpoint to her breath. She pushes back hard, testing, driving, forcing me to meet her pace. My grip tightens, not to control but to answer, keep us synced. Her body takes every adjustment—when I angle higher, she moans low; when I circle her with my thumb, she loses coherence, collapsing forward onto her arms.

Her voice is wrecked now, sounds torn from her instead of chosen. It spikes through me like voltage, every cry pushing me closer. My thighs tremble with the strain of holding steady, chest tight, sweat running down my spine.

"Feel good?" I manage, not fishing—confirming.

"Yes," she chokes, immediate. Raw. "Don't stop."

"Not planning to." Flat truth.

I keep one hand clamped on her hip, the other circling where she's hottest. The reaction is instant: her spine bows, her shoulders sag, and the cry she gives me is guttural enough to mark the edge.

"Come for me," I say, measured, steady.

She does—hard, whole body seizing, head tossing back, her voice ripped clean out of her throat. The pulsing grip around me drags me under with her. My release breaks, hips driving through each convulsion until I'm spent, braced over her, shaking with the effort of control.

She collapses forward, cheek pressed to the pillow, body still shivering. I stay braced over her for a breath, then ease down beside her, one arm circling to draw her back against my chest. Her skin is slick with heat, pulse racing under my palm where it rests low on her stomach.

"Breathe," I murmur, more suggestion than command. Her chest rises uneven, then steadies into my rhythm. Small tells line up: the tremor in her thighs, fingers knotting in the sheet then unclenching, the rasp in her throat when she sighs.

I press a kiss between her shoulder blades. Not strategy—instinct. She softens under it, eyelids heavy, but

I can feel the hum still running through her. Not finished.

My own body's cooling, the hard edge gone, but when she shifts—hips rolling back just enough to brush me—the spark kicks sharp and insistent. Not ready yet, but she's testing.

"Kitty Cat," I murmur, warning and question at once.

She glances back, eyes half-lidded, mouth curved wrecked but certain. She moves again, slower, deliberate. Heat stirs low, blood answering before logic can.

Her fingertips trail my ribs, feather-light. I shift but don't stop her. A smile tugs unplanned at my mouth, eyes slitting open.

"You're insatiable," I rasp—rough, amused.

"Maybe." Her voice is wrecked, raw. "But I don't think I'm done with you yet."

I huff a laugh, half-doubtful, half-pleased. My body's soft against her hip, spent. Real. She hesitates—but curiosity wins. Her hand slides lower, circling, not pushing.

At first, nothing. Just warmth and the twitch of muscles coming down. But when she bends to kiss my chest, mouth tracing damp skin, a sharper breath rips out of me. Her nails graze my stomach and I catch again, rougher.

It's not instant. It shouldn't be. But every pass of her lips, every press of her palm coaxes me. Gradual, shy almost—soft turning to firm, then fuller, heavier in her hand. My eyes snap open, focus sharpening like I hadn't believed it possible.

"Kitty Cat..." My voice is a rasp—warning, wonder, both.

She looks up through her lashes, hand still moving. "Told you I wasn't finished."

The disbelief drains, hunger taking its place. I close my hand over hers—not to stop, but to steady, to press firmer. Heat rushes under her palm, my chest climbing faster. The impossible turns inevitable.

The spark—already reckless—ignites again. She pushes, steady and insistent. I follow.

She swings a leg over and straddles me, skin to skin this time, nothing between us. Heat presses down, slick and insistent, and my body answers fast—blood rushing, thickening under the drag of her grind. My breath punches out sharp.

Her eyes flash as she reaches for the nightstand—wrapper, quick and steady; she rolls a fresh
one on me herself. That single act—decisive, deliberate—nearly finishes me before we've even started.

She sinks down slow, inch by inch, and the stretch
makes my jaw clamp tight. She's hot, gripping, perfect, and the sound she makes as she takes me fully—wrecked, raw—is one I'll keep replaying.

Her breasts sway above me, full and flushed, every
rise and fall of her rhythm drawing my eyes. I reach
up, cup one, thumb circling the peaked tip. Her gasp
shudders through her whole frame, and she arches
harder into my palm.

She sets the pace, hips rolling, finding her rhythm. I
let her, mapping each tell: the way her breath stutters
when she leans forward, the sharp sound she makes
when she grinds down harder, the nails digging crescents into my chest when I thrust up to meet her.

"Christ," I rasp, hands gripping her waist, guiding
just enough to keep us synced. She's wild above me,
wrecked and unguarded, every motion pulling me
tighter, and the sight alone is almost enough.

Her pace builds, body winding tighter, breasts
bouncing with each drive. I mouth one, sucking,

teeth grazing lightly, and she breaks on a sobbed moan, clamping around me. The pulse drags me over with her, my release tearing out in deep, shuddering thrusts until there's nothing left but the sound of us, wrecked and breathing each other's air.

I hold her down against me, hands steady at her hips, eyes locked on her face. This isn't theory. This isn't chance. It's real.

She collapses forward onto my chest, skin slick, breasts flattened against me, heartbeat pounding hard enough I can feel it through bone.

I wrap my arms around her, one at her back, the other sliding up to the nape of her neck. She fits there, trembling but safe, breath ragged against my throat. I murmur quiet things without thinking—"breathe," "I've got you"—words I don't usually spend but feel right here.

Her pulse slows, breaths evening out. The tremors fade into little aftershocks that roll through her thighs now and then. My own heart steadies against hers, slower but no less strong.

She shifts once, barely, like she means to speak. Instead her body just melts heavier into mine, her cheek pressing into my shoulder. Her hand flattens over my chest, palm warm, fingers twitching once before going still.

Sleep takes her fast. I can tell by the way her body lets go completely, weight settling into me instead of holding itself. The little cat ears she never pulled off are crooked, barely hanging on, and the sight punches a quiet smile out of me.

I stay still, not daring to move, cataloging details: the scent of her hair damp with sweat, the heat radiating off her skin, the complete lack of guard in her face. Trust, total. That's what this is. That's what undoes me more than anything else tonight.

But dawn is closer than I want. Routine doesn't wait. Lily doesn't wait. I'll need to move soon, make the shift from this pocket back to the life that anchors me.

Not yet. For now, I hold her tighter, let her breathing guide mine, and let the rare quiet stretch as long as I can.

⁂

Dawn smears faint light past the curtains when my eyes open. She's still curled into me—hair tangled, breath steady, the covers kicked halfway down so her bare shoulder is warm against my chest. Peace looks good on her. Fragile. Rare.

I let myself stay there one more minute. Just feel it: her hand spread over my ribs, her leg hooked across mine, the kind of weight that says she trusted me enough to sleep without guard. That's not something I take lightly.

But the clock doesn't care. Lily's morning is non-negotiable. I ease out slow, careful not to wake her. She murmurs once, shifts deeper into the pillow, then goes quiet again.

I clean up, dress, and write a note—brief, tidy, all I can give with the time I've got:

Kat— Had an amazing night. Sorry to leave early. I'll call you later. —E.J.

I tuck it under her bag where she'll see it. One last look: she's still asleep, lashes shadowing her cheeks, the mask ears finally askew on the nightstand. Then I go.

The hotel hallway is hushed. The city air outside snaps cool against my face, cutting through the fog of the night. Compartment shift: romance closed, dad mode open.

Sam's porch still wears plastic ghosts and a lopsided pumpkin. She opens the door, raises a brow at my rumpled clothes and whatever's written on my face.

"Rough night? Or a really good one?"

"Better than good," I answer, dry enough that she grins.

"Later," she says, meaning tell me everything, and steps aside.

Then: "Daddy!"

Lily barrels into my arms. The hug resets everything. Candy breath, backpack bounce, arms tight around my neck—this is the axis the rest of my life spins on. She launches into a play-by-play of the night, enthusiasm at full volume. My brain kicks into overclocked mode trying to keep up, running parallel processes just to decode the timeline.

Drop-off is autopilot—songs in the car, her voice off-key and bright, then the little wave-and-run toward the school doors. I sit for a moment longer than usual, hands loose on the wheel, the echo of last night running parallel with the solidity of this morning.

They don't cancel each other. They stack. Anchor and spark. Duty and desire. Both true.

I pull into traffic with a plan forming: call her—tonight. Test if the signal repeats. Not fate. Not noise. Pattern. Strong enough to follow.

CHAPTER 9
Notes & Noise

Kat on paper. Ache in your chest.

SCARLETT

A soft, gold wash presses against my eyelids. I don't open them right away—I stretch first, toes curling under sheets, chest loose in the kind of warmth that still clings from last night. His hands, his voice, the weight of him steady above me—it hums through my body like residue. A smile tugs before I can stop it. I roll, reaching across the bed to find him.

Cold.

The dip in the mattress is hollow, the sheets cool. The lurch comes fast, low in my gut, before thought can catch up. My eyes snap open. The other side is rumpled but empty. No clothes on the chair. No boots by the wall. His overnight bag—gone.

The air feels scrubbed, silence too neat, like the room reset itself while I slept. Same bed, same view—but it doesn't feel like the same place. The champagne sweats in melted ice; one glass lies on its side. The city beyond the glass wall is dull where last night it burned.

I sit up too quickly, the sheet dragging against bare skin. Suspicion prickles, then hollows out. That's when I see it—a slip of paper half-tucked beneath my black bag. My fingers shake as I pull it free.

Kat, I had an amazing night. Sorry I had to leave so early. I'll call you later. —E.J.

Kat. Not Cat.

All night I told myself he was being playful, costume-cute. Written, it isn't a joke—it's a name. Not mine.

Heat stings my face. The memories unspool too fast: his eyes steady on mine, the way he asked about kids like the answer mattered, the patience in his hands. They flicker now like tricks of light, flimsy, like maybe they belonged to someone else. To Kat.

I drag the catsuit back on because it's all I have. Last night it was a key in the right lock—Halloween noise outside, mask and ears making sense. This morning the lock has changed. Latex clings wrong, itchy, every seam exposed by daylight. In the mirror I catch a girl with smudged eyes, hair tangled, cleavage framed in black that doesn't feel like mine.

Not Kitty Cat. Not Scarlett. Just someone playing dress-up.

I almost grab the little mask, but I don't. I slide the note into my bag and walk out.

The hallway hums with ordinary life—housekeeper wheeling a cart, a couple with coffee and matching sweatshirts waiting for the elevator. Everyone seems fitted into their morning. I move through them like a ghost, latex creaking faintly, wrong in the light.

The lobby is colder by daylight. My Uber pings; I slip into the back seat and fold my hands in my lap. The driver says nothing; I'm grateful. The city scrolls by—joggers at crosswalks, bakery windows glowing, the smell of bread I can't taste. Each reminder of routine presses the ache deeper, settling heavy and low.

By the time I'm on our stairs, I'm hollowed out. I ease the door open, aiming for my room. Tessa is curled on the couch, blanket bunched at her waist, hair in a messy pile. She stirs as the door clicks shut, blinking against the light.

"Scar?" she says, voice thick with sleep. "You're just getting in?"

Her eyes find my outfit, and the smile that tries to rise dies fast.

"Yeah." The word scrapes.

"That must've been—" She breaks off, squints. "Oh. Hey. Come here."

I don't mean to, but my knees bend anyway. I cross to her, latex and all, and the tears I held on the elevator and in the car and up the stairwell finally break. She wraps me up and lets me shake against her T-shirt until my ribs stop shuddering.

When I can breathe again, I scrub my face with the heel of my hand. "Sorry."

"Don't you dare," she says, already rising. "Coffee. Clothes. Then you talk; I listen."

I nod and slip toward my room. The catsuit peels off with a sticky sound and puddles on the floor like a bad idea. I leave it there.

I come back in leggings and an oversized sweatshirt, hair damp from splashing water on my face. The suit lies crumpled on my floor, where it belongs.

Tessa has two mugs waiting. Steam lifts in pale curls, coffee's sharp bite cutting the last trace of that costume from my throat. I sink into the couch beside her, ceramic hot against my palms. The warmth helps. The hollow doesn't.

She tucks one leg under herself and waits. Doesn't push. Just watches until the words find me.

"They had trivia," I say, fingers tight around the mug. "Costumes everywhere, noise that was too much at first. But then..." I swallow. "He found me. And it eased. Trivia, the maze—we just—" The word sticks. "We fit. I grabbed his arm once, and he didn't pull away. He just... steadied me. Like it was the most natural thing."

She doesn't interrupt. Just watches, eyes soft, tracking more than what I'm saying.

"There was a kiss." My voice dips, barely carrying. "And then later, the room." Heat prickles my cheeks. "I don't do that, Tess. I don't. But I did. With him."

What I really mean hums under it: *I trusted him. I opened in ways I don't.*

I circle the rim of the mug with my thumb, steam curling and vanishing. "It wasn't casual," I add, the words pushed out like they've been waiting. "He asked about kids. Like it mattered."

My chest tightens. "And I believed him. I let myself believe."

Silence folds in—not empty. Tessa's presence stays steady, grounding.

"And then I woke up alone." I reach into my bag, unfold the slip, and smooth it on my knee.

She leans in. Her eyes skim, then snag. Her mouth twists. "Kat."

The word slices fresh.

"All night I told myself he meant Cat," I manage. "Costume-playful. A joke. But this... Kat isn't me. It isn't anyone I showed him. Not Scarlett. Not Kitty Cat. Someone else altogether."

Her gaze holds mine. "If the only thing wrong here is a name, that's not fatal. That's fixable."

My stomach twists. "Don't. That makes it worse—like I stole someone else's night by mistake."

"Or," she says gently, "you turned a night meant for someone else into yours. The version that mattered was you."

Her hand covers mine, thumb drawing slow circles. I stare at the steam. The ache doesn't vanish, but its edge dulls. A thin, stubborn sliver pries through anyway.

"Maybe I should just let it go," I whisper. "File it under a good memory and move on."

"You don't believe that."

"I want to." The words land heavy. "I should. But last night felt... different. Like more than pretend. And I can't shake it."

"Then don't," she says simply. "If it's real, it won't evaporate because morning came. He left a note. That means something."

I press the rim of the mug to my lip. "I didn't even tell him my name. I let him call me the wrong thing because it felt easier than correcting him."

"That's so you," Tessa says gently. "Keeping the moment smooth instead of correcting him. But that doesn't mean you weren't fully there. And if the mistake is the name he thought you went by—not the person you were with him—then the truth is, he already knew *you* without knowing it."

I look down at the note. The letters blur, clear again. The sting of my own silence sits beside the hurt he left. Both true.

"I don't know how this ends," I admit. "But I don't think it's over."

Her smile says she knew I'd land there. "Then we'll be ready when the universe hands you a clue. In the meantime? Breakfast sandwiches. And a long shower to wash the latex out of your pores."

"God, yes." I set the mug down, tip my head back. "And maybe later I'll pick the suit off my floor."

"Leave it there. Let it think about what it's done."

A laugh slips out, shaky but real. The hurt is still inside me, but so is the echo of his steadiness, the way last night shifted my breath—the flicker of something I can't name and won't let go of.

But underneath the hurt, one truth keeps humming: it isn't over.

CHAPTER 10
Glitches & Grit

Wrong setup. Right connection. Don't stop.

ELI

Morning glare cuts across the dash. I'm still running hot from her—the way she fit against me, the sound she made when I pressed just right. Normally by now I'd have night in one box, day in another. But this won't file. It hums like live current under my ribs. Signal, not noise.

The house hits with contrast—candy wrappers on the table, glitter on the couch, decorations sagging. Ordinary chaos. But it doesn't absorb me. I strip fast, step into the shower, let heat hammer my shoulders. Her face still reels behind my eyes: the spark in her laugh, the steadiness in her gaze, the way her body answered me like calibration landing exact. My breath catches, rough. That wasn't luck. It was alignment. Rare. The kind you don't ignore.

The towel is barely knotted at my waist when I thumb his number. No time to wait. Straight to the one who set this up. Connor answers on the third ring, voice bright, too casual.

"E.J.! There he is. How'd it go?"

His cheer needles. Too light against the edge running under my skin. I push past it. "I owe you. Send me her number."

A chuckle, lazy. "Whoa, whoa. You know the rules—no freebies. Details first."

My grip tightens on the phone. "Connor. Number."

He drags it out, enjoying himself. "At least tell me this—what'd Kat end up in? The kitten thing work out?"

"Catwoman," I say. The word lands flat.

There's a pause—long enough to register wrong. Then: "Wait. Catwoman?"

"Yes." My tone sharpens before I can blunt it. The silence on his end stretches, brittle.

"E.J...." He gives a nervous laugh. "Kat wasn't Catwoman. She told me—sex kitten. Leotard, garters. Not latex."

For a second, sound narrows. My chest locks tight. Grip hardens until the phone creaks. Input doesn't match output. The assumption fails.

"You're telling me I was with a stranger last night?"

"Unless I'm crazy—yeah. Kat's not subtle. She'd never cover up. Not like that."

The words hit like an alarm. Pressure climbs under my sternum. Not Kat. Not the setup. A woman I don't know. No name. No number. Just a note meant for someone else.

I force my voice steady. "What exactly did you tell her?"

"That she'd find you at eight. Lone Ranger, right?"

I shut my eyes, heat scraping up my throat. "Connor. I was Zorro. Not the Lone Ranger."

He scoffs. "Same diff."

"No." The word comes sharp. "It isn't. That difference cost me her name. Her number. Maybe everything."

The image spikes: her waking alone, finding the wrong name scrawled under her bag. My error. Preventable.

The pressure bears down, but under it a cleaner line cuts through: resolve.

I end the call. No wasted cycles. The system failed. Adapt.

The call with Connor leaves a hollow thud in my chest. I'm halfway into my work clothes—slacks, button-up, the armor of order—when I stop. Laptop bag waiting by the door. Calendar pinging on my phone. Routine tugging hard.

I set the bag down. Not today.

Skipping work isn't me. Variables pile up when you leave your post. But if I wait, the trail goes cold. If I move now, there's still a chance. The system adjusts.

Hotel first. Polite refusals. Privacy policies. No progress. I log off fast, jaw tight.

Social next. Geotags, hashtags, timestamps. Hundreds of shots. Masks, glitter, blurred outlines. My pulse jumps at a shadow of her hair, the slope of a shoulder—then crashes when the angle proves wrong. Nothing.

Hours pass. My inbox fills. I ignore it. Each failed filter feels like chasing a signal that dissolves the second I touch it.

And under the frustration, a sharper question needles: why didn't she tell me? Her real name. She let me call her Kat, let it ride all night. Playful? Avoidance? Did she not trust me enough to risk the correction? Or did she think it didn't matter?

The thought gnaws. I shove it aside. Action, not speculation.

I grab my keys and drive. Gravel crunches under my tires when I pull up to Sam's.

She opens the door, eyebrows up. "Eli? Shouldn't you be at work?"

"I need your help." The words land heavier than I intend.

Her expression shifts, the easy humor softening into something steadier. "Okay. Come in."

I step past into her living room—crayon drawings layered on the fridge, some Lily's, some clearly her boys', names half-visible under thick marker swirls. A scatter of toys crowds the corner, colors clashing. Not my house—but part of my rhythm, my anchor. Evidence of the life that grounds me.

I lay it out: wrong setup, wrong woman, right connection. No name. No number. Just a note addressed to someone else.

Sam listens, arms crossed, weight on one hip. Not mocking, not pitying—just absorbing.

When I finish, the silence stretches. Then: "You're serious about this."

"Yeah." My voice roughens. "I am."

Her mouth curves—not a grin, something smaller. Warmer. "Alright. I'll dig. Hotel, socials, whatever I can reach. We'll find her."

Relief cuts hard, immediate, almost dizzying. "Thanks, Sam."

She waves it off. "Don't thank me yet. Just promise me if I find her, you won't blow it."

The corner of my mouth lifts, automatic. "I won't."

Back in the car, the ache hasn't gone. But it's shifted—less despair, more determination. Work will wait. This can't.

The first week, I comb hashtags and geotags, filter by location and timestamp, zoom in on blurred faces at the edge of other people's party photos. Nothing.

The second, I cross-reference upload times, usernames, private accounts. Silence. Even Sam's contacts hit walls.

By the third, the ache behind my ribs has settled in permanent, a constant pressure. Each dead end sharpens the same truth: she's out there, and I let her walk away without a name.

Most men would take the hint. Call it chance. Move on.

That's not how I'm wired. Rare signals don't come twice.

So I keep going.

CHAPTER 11
Late & Certain

Two lines. One truth you choose.

SCARLETT

Plastic pumpkins collapse into garbage bags. The air thins, sharper at the edges. Coffee shops trade spiderwebs for paper turkeys. The whole city pivots, and I'm still stuck on repeat.

Each morning I check my phone like muscle memory, as if some unknown number might appear, carrying him on the other end. Each night I scroll the hotel hashtag until the photos blur—same costumes, same faces, never him. Twice I called the front desk, voice shaking; the third time I hung up before anyone answered.

The apartment is too quiet now. With Tessa away at her family's for Thanksgiving, the silence feels heavy, almost solid. I flick the TV on just to break it, but the voices don't stick. The silence seeps under anyway.

I curl into the couch, blanket to my chin, staring at nothing while the weight in my chest spreads wider. Out there, the world's moved on—candles swapped for cranberries, streets dressed for the next holiday. In here, I'm still circling one night, one man, like a puzzle I can't solve.

When I close my eyes, I'm back there.

The hotel room glowing with city light through the windows, shadows flickering as we moved. My pulse tripping until he looked at me—steady, certain—and everything inside me eased. His voice low at my ear, each touch careful but sure. The way he held me like I wasn't a risk he had to calculate but a choice he'd already made.

And me—God, me—leaning in, saying yes with every breath, every shift of my body. Letting go in a way I never do. A version of myself I don't hand out. I gave it to him.

But the loop never stops there. It always breaks on the cold space beside me, the sheets smoothed flat where his body should've been. The note tucked under my bag with someone else's name on it. *Kat.*

I jolt, eyes flying open, the throw fisted at my chest. The room around me is dim and ordinary—half-washed mugs in the sink, books stacked lopsided on the table. Safe. Normal. Nothing like the fire I keep replaying. And still my body hums with it, like memory alone can drag me back.

The ache in my chest isn't the only thing that won't settle. My stomach twists again, sharp this time, and I press a hand flat against it. At first I told myself it was stress—too many nights running loops in my head, too little sleep, too much coffee. Easy culprit.

But the nausea keeps rolling back. Stronger now. Relentless.

I sit forward, elbows braced on my knees, trying to breathe through it. My mind reaches for patterns, little anchors. We were careful. Every time. Condoms.

No slip, no break. The facts line up neat, but my body isn't listening.

My fingers curl tighter in the blanket. I start counting backward, calendar pages flipping in my head. Days. Then more. Two weeks late.

The realization doesn't crash in. It clicks shut—clean, irrevocable—like a door slamming in my mind. My throat goes dry.

No. No, that can't—

But it can.

The word rises, silent and brutal: *pregnant.*

I force myself upright, blanket sliding off, skin clammy. My purse waits by the door; I grab it like it might anchor me. The pharmacy is only three blocks, but each step feels wrong-footed, like walking on a street I don't recognize.

The bag crinkles in my hand on the way back, ordinary sound against the storm inside.

In the bathroom I tear the box open too fast, cardboard ripping. My hands shake as I read the instructions twice, then a third time, as if clarity is hidden in the margins. I follow the steps anyway.

Minutes drag heavy. Each second stretches, thick and slow, like watching wax drip from a candle. My eyes fix on the counter but not really—everything blurs.

Then the result sharpens, bold and undeniable.

Positive.

Air punches out of me. My hand clamps over my mouth. My knees give, and I sink to the tile, the test still clutched in my fist.

The word *careless* hisses in my head. How could I let this happen? Panic claws hard, but underneath, something quieter stirs—impossible, insistent. Certainty.

I want this baby.

The thought shocks me even as it lands, but once it does, it roots deep, immovable.

The phone buzzes across the coffee table. Mom. For months I've let calls like this slide to voicemail the ache still too sharp from August—her whirlwind marriage, running off with a man she'd barely known.

It had felt reckless, like she'd traded our history for something shiny and sudden.

My thumb hesitates, then betrays me. I swipe.

Her voice comes warm, too bright for the quiet of my apartment. She talks about Thanksgiving dinner, about Richard's kids and grandkids, about how I'd "really love them." I sit there with the test still on the counter, murmuring replies, the words catching in my throat.

All this time I've judged her for leaping into love without a plan. But now—I know what that pull feels like. The sense of recognition so strong it makes reason irrelevant. The reckless part doesn't vanish, but for the first time I can imagine how it might also feel like certainty.

I close my eyes and listen. The ache between us is still there, but under it flickers something new: the thought that I don't have to do this alone. She would help me. Richard's family might too. Support is there, waiting, if I just step toward it.

When we hang up, I set the phone in my lap and exhale. Fear still sits heavy, but the decision clicks clean and certain in its place. I'll go to Thanksgiving. I'll see her. I'll meet them.

Not because the fear is gone, but because I can't carry this alone anymore.

I press a hand to my stomach, the weight of the decision settling in. Whoever he was—whoever he is—he's not here. But I am. And I won't be alone.

Resolve settles in. I'll go—and I'll step into it.

But under it, the ache hums steady: that night still matters. And I can't let it go.

CHAPTER 12
Thresholds & Recognition

The search ends at the door.

ELI

The house smells like Thanksgiving—roast turkey, cinnamon, warm bread. Most people sink into that. For me, it lands off-center.

Patricia opens the door, bright already. Lily bounces on her toes, holding out the bouquet she picked, and Patricia scoops her up, cooing over the flowers. My chest tugs. Patricia's been a soft place for Lily to land. I'll never take that for granted. But even here, surrounded by family, the absence presses in—rumpled sheets, a note with the wrong name, hotel calls, hashtags, dead ends.

Dad's voice cuts across the threshold. "Still no luck?"

"Not yet." I keep it clipped. No room for the truth. And still I can't stop.

The house hums with life—Sam's laugh from the kitchen, football on TV, silverware clattering as Lily sets a place under Patricia's guidance. I stand too long in the doorway, imagining auburn hair catching the chandelier light, a place set for someone who isn't here.

The doorbell rings.

Patricia brightens. "Oh! That must be her."

Lily perks, eyes shining, too much energy to keep still. "Can I get it? Please, Daddy?"

"Come on." I scoop her up, carry her toward the foyer. My skin prickles. System bracing for reset.

She's framed by cold light, shoulders drawn tight in a simple wool coat, auburn hair tucked behind one ear. Her hand grips the strap of her bag, knuckles pale. Not made up, not masked. Just her.

For a beat my brain refuses to accept it. Weeks of dead ends, hotel calls, hashtags, sleepless replay—every scenario but this. And yet—every data point: eyes wide, lips parted, chest rising fast. Memory aligns. Reality slams home.

Not a ghost. Not a trick. Her.

Relief crashes so hard it feels like pain, ribs pried open around the first clean breath in a month.

The pause stretches.

Then—

"E.J.?" she whispers.

My throat locks. My mouth finds the only name I've had. "Kitty Cat?"

Her lips curve, tremble, steady. "It's actually Scarlett."

Scarlett. The name lands like a final puzzle piece. What I chased wasn't a phantom—it was her. Standing in my father's doorway.

Lily wriggles free and darts straight to her, small hand catching Scarlett's fingers like it's instinct. "Are you going to eat turkey with us?"

Scarlett kneels, smile flickering but warm. "I sure am."

The sight punches air into my lungs. She's here.

When Lily darts away again, I catch Scarlett's hand and tug her down the hall. The guest room door clicks shut.

For a moment we just stare, breath loud in the silence. Weeks of chasing shadows, every lead collapsing into nothing—and now she's here, not imagined, not lost. Probability says impossible. My pulse says inevitable.

Restraint fractures. My mouth finds hers, the kiss hard, weeks of frustration and longing detonating at once. She meets me with equal force. For a moment, the world rights itself.

I break just enough to breathe, forehead pressed to hers. For weeks she was only memory, a ghost I tried to convince myself I'd imagined. But she's right here. Solid. Breathing. Real.

Her eyes shimmer as she pulls back just enough for words. Fear flickers there. "I thought you left me."

CHAPTER 13

Catch & Crack

You say the fear out loud. He stays.

SCARLETT

His kiss lingers, aching, but the words I just let slip hang heavier than anything else. *I thought you left me.*

For a heartbeat he just looks at me, his hand still cupping my jaw. And I really see him for the first time—no mask, no blur of shadows. Broad shoulders framed in the light, dark hair a little mussed, a button-down rolled to his forearms, veins standing out as he holds me tighter. His mouth parted, breath uneven. And his eyes—steady, storm-dark, raw with something I don't dare name.

"I didn't leave you," he says finally, voice low, rougher than it was that night. "I never meant that to be the end."

The calm in his face should be enough, but my chest squeezes harder. Because I've been holding something heavier still, and it pounds against my ribs now, demanding out.

I drop my gaze, nails biting into my palm. "I..." My mouth is dry. My tongue sticks. Tears rise faster than words, spilling hot before I can hold them back.

He pulls me in tight, misunderstanding. "I tried to find you."

I shake my head, but the sound that comes out is only a broken sob. I press my face into his chest, refusing to meet his eyes.

He tilts my chin up, firm, forcing me to see him. "Look at me, Scarlett. You have to believe me."

My lips tremble. Finally, I manage a whisper, jagged through tears. "It's not that."

His brows knit, tension carved sharp across his face. "Then what is it?"

"I... I can't," I stammer, voice cracking, retreat pressing at the edges of my tongue.

"Scarlett." His tone sharpens—not harsh, but steady as stone. "Whatever it is, you can tell me."

His thumb strokes my wrist, patient, even. That patience is what undoes me.

The words scrape raw, jagged, like glass tearing free of my throat. "I'm pregnant."

CHAPTER 14

Shock & Steady

Fear is noise. Resolve is the answer.

ELI

Pregnant. The word detonates.

For a second, the system blanks—no airflow, no signal, just her face tilted up to mine, eyes wet and terrified. My mind scrambles to spin the inputs into order: we used protection, safeguards every time. Still, the data point sits there, fixed, undeniable.

I tighten my grip on her wrist, grounding us both. "Say it again," I manage. Not because I doubt her—I don't. Because hearing it once shocked me. Hearing it again lets me feel it.

Her chin trembles, but she doesn't look away. "I'm pregnant."

There it is. No theory. No simulation. Reality.

The floor steadies and tilts at once. In the span of a breath, a cascade: Lily's laugh, her backpack bouncing on a school morning. Evenings of homework, mornings of pancakes. And now—another heartbeat folded into that future. Hers. Ours.

Fear should dominate. Logistics, disruption, unknowns. Instead, what rises is sharper: resolve.

I shift, cup her face, make her see me. Her tears streak warm across my thumb. "Scarlett," I say, low, even. "You're not alone in this. You won't do it alone."

She shakes her head, voice breaking. "I was so afraid you'd—"

"I won't." Final. No space for doubt. "I never meant to leave you, and I'm not leaving you now."

Her breath hitches, a sound caught between sob and release, and she folds into me. I hold her tight, chest to chest, feeling the quake in her body start to ease.

For weeks I'd been searching blind, chasing ghosts through hashtags and hotel registries. All along, the real signal wasn't out there. It was here—close, constant, just out of frame.

The path forward is still fog. But this much I know: she isn't a ghost anymore. She's real. And we're already in it. Together.

Her tears are still fresh on her cheeks, damp against my shirt, when the door creaks open.

"Eli, for the love of—" Sam's voice slices in, then cuts short. She blinks at us—Scarlett still flushed, eyes red—and her expression jolts from sass to curiosity in half a second.

Scarlett jerks back, eyes wide, color rushing her cheeks. I turn. Sam stands frozen in the doorway, staring like she's stumbled into a soap opera.

Silence, charged.

I squeeze Scarlett's hand, anchoring her. "Good news," I say evenly. "I found Kat."

Sam blinks once. Twice. Then her face splits wide open. "Wait. Kat is... Scarlett? Patricia's Scarlett?"

Scarlett swallows, her voice small but steady. "Yeah. Surprise."

Sam bursts into laughter—bright, unfiltered. She steps in, hand shooting out to Scarlett. "Scarlett, hi. I'm Sam—Eli's sister, Lily's aunt, resident chaos co-ordinator. And oh my God, you have no idea how badly I've been dying to meet you."

Scarlett takes her hand, still flushed, but there's the faintest tug of a smile.

Sam barrels on, eyes flicking between us. "Do you know this man has been driving us insane for the last month? Calls to the hotel, stalking hashtags, dragging me into midnight internet dives. He's been a lovesick detective without a case file. And it was you. Here. All along."

Scarlett's eyes cut to me—mortified, but softening. Proof.

Sam claps her hands. "Alright, lovebirds. Enough hiding. You're coming out there with me, and we're telling everyone."

Scarlett hesitates. I squeeze her hand—steady. She exhales, releases it.

Sam loops an arm through hers, already tugging toward the hall. Scarlett glances back at me, wide-eyed, but hope flickers beneath it.

I fall into step beside her. And when her hand reaches for mine again, I don't hesitate. I take it.

The warmth of Thanksgiving rolls over us—turkey roasting, pies cooling, football murmuring on the TV. Family noise, ordinary and full. Except nothing about this moment is ordinary.

Sam barrels ahead, tugging Scarlett toward the living room. My hand stays locked around hers, our grip giving us away before either of us says a word.

Patricia looks up first. Her smile is automatic, bright—until she sees our hands. It falters into a sharp little gasp.

Dad's brows climb. Mark lets out a low whistle. A ripple moves through the room, realization catching from one face to the next.

Scarlett's shoulders square, but I can feel the tremor in her palm. I keep hold, steadying her.

Lily's voice slices the silence. "Daddy?"

I drop to her level. "Yes, sweetheart?"

Her eyes—so serious, too big for her face—flick between Scarlett and me. "Is she the one you were looking for?"

My chest tightens. Instinct says protect her. But she deserves the truth. I meet her eyes. "Yes, Lily. This is Scarlett. She's the one."

Scarlett stiffens beside me, breath catching sharp. Her shoulders square again, tremor running through her palm as she answers.

Lily lights up, guileless joy spilling across her face. She barrels straight into Scarlett's waist, arms wrapping tight. "You're her! Daddy's been looking for you forever!"

Scarlett laughs, shaky, crouching to return the hug. "I guess I am. I'm so glad to meet you, Lily."

Emotion surges up my chest, raw and hot. Harder to contain than anything I've felt in years.

Then Lily leans back, tilts her head, and asks the question that freezes the room. "Are you gonna be my mommy?"

My throat locks. Instinct says protect her—shield her from too much, too soon. My eyes lock with Scarlett's. She's wide-eyed, stunned, but her answer comes gentle, sure. "I don't know yet, sweetheart. But I do know I care about your daddy very much. And I'd love to get to know you better."

Lily nods, satisfied, whispering something in Scarlett's ear that makes her smile bloom real and bright.

The room exhales at once—Patricia swiping at her eyes, Dad muttering "Well, damn," Sam grinning like she orchestrated the whole thing. Family noise starts back up, laughter and plates clattering, but it feels fragile—like glass that could crack with one wrong move.

Laughter and background noise blur together. Under it sits the truth we haven't said—the kind that fractures rooms. This was the easy part. The hard part is next.

CHAPTER 15
Knots & Confession

Best friends hold what you can't carry alone.

SCARLETT

The apartment feels too small for how heavy my chest is. My steps drag grooves into the floorboards, breath hitching every turn.

Lily's voice won't stop ringing—*Are you gonna be my mommy?* It echoes like a bell that won't fade, her kid-shampoo scent and cinnamon-pie warmth still clinging to my sweater. It should have steadied me. Instead, it cracked me wide, ribs pried apart from the inside.

The lock rattles. My body seizes, breath spiking sharp. Tessa's here. Relief collides with dread in my chest—I've been waiting for this, needing her, and now I have to say it all out loud.

"Honey, I'm home!" Tessa sing-songs, suitcase bumping the threshold. She drops inside in one of those whirlwind entrances: strawberry-blonde hair piled in a messy topknot, green eyes bright, a threadbare jacket slung over one shoulder.

My knees go loose, like someone cut the cord. Before I can think, I cross the room too fast, arms flinging around her. The press of her coat against my cheek is rough, grounding.

She laughs into my hair, startled. Then stiffens. "Miss me that much?" The joke thins, edges sharpening. "Scar?"

Heat surges in my face; my chest seizes tight. His mouth in that guest room doorway flashes behind my eyes—oxygen after drowning—then Lily's question slices through again, tearing the air from me.

I pull back, fingers clutching the hem of my sweatshirt. "I need to talk to you." My voice scrapes thin, papery.

Her eyes narrow, attuned. She kicks the suitcase aside and drops onto the couch, tucking one leg under. "Okay. Spill."

I sink down beside her, bones jittering. My hands twist together until the knuckles burn. *Say it. Or swallow it.*

"Remember E.J.?"

She groans, rolling her eyes. "Mr. Hot Halloween? The one you've been pining and raging over in alternating shifts? Vividly."

Blood rushes hot under my skin; my lip finds my teeth. "I found him."

Her head snaps up. "No. Way. You did?"

My stomach flips cold. My nails dig crescents into my palms. Air feels sour in my chest. They all saw it. Mom hugging me. Him saying my name. He didn't find Kat. He found me.

"Yeah," I manage. "But his name isn't E.J. It's Eli. Eli Carrington."

Her brows knit, suspicion catching. "Carrington. As in... your mom's new husband?"

My throat locks, pulse beating hard at the hinge of my jaw. "Yeah." My voice falls to a whisper. "He's my stepbrother."

Silence. Her mouth drops. "Scarlett. Wow. Okay. Straight out of a soap opera."

A laugh jerks out, brittle, wrong. "Tell me about it."

Her gaze steadies, sharp now. "And you're telling me this like it's the smaller bomb. Which means..."

Sweat slicks my palms. I press them flat to my knees, but the tremor won't stop. My chest claws for air. "There's more."

She leans in, hand covering mine—warm, solid, unyielding.

My ribs cave, heart ricocheting up my throat. Say it—my mind hammers. My breath shatters, and the words rip free—"I'm pregnant."

Her eyes widen, blinking once, twice. Her grip tightens. "Pregnant?"

Tears burn, spill hot across my cheeks. I nod. "I found out before Thanksgiving. He knows. You're the first person I've told besides him."

Mom's hug flashes through me—her arms tight, her eyes damp. I smiled back with a secret thrumming under my ribs. Wrong to hide. Necessary. For now.

Tessa exhales hard, then pulls me straight into her arms. The hug is fierce, unshakable. "Okay. Okay. You're not alone in this. You've got me."

My ribs quake against her shoulder, but the choke-hold on my lungs loosens, like a knot giving way thread by thread.

She leans back, wiping her eyes with a shaky laugh. "Guess that makes me Aunt Tessa. God help us."

A laugh sputters out of me too, strangled but real. "Yeah."

Her grip clamps firmer. "Listen. You're gonna be an incredible mom. And I'll be here—nagging, cheering, spoiling the kid rotten. Always."

My muscles give, slack with sudden release. Shoulders drop; breath flows easier than it has in weeks. For the first time, my chest expands without ache—

but the thought spikes sharp anyway: incredible moms don't usually start with secrets this big.

CHAPTER 16
Lists & Presence

Plan the day. Show up for her.

ELI

Saturday morning. The house is weekend-soft, coffee steam curling on the counter.

Lily sprawls on the rug, dolls lined like recruits. Her hair keeps falling forward; she pushes it back, then sneaks a glance at me to check I'm watching.

I try to return to the laptop. Monday's files glare, calendar alerts ping like gnats. None of it sticks. My focus drags back to Scarlett—the way she whispered it. Pregnant. Her eyes wet, throat trembling. The weight of Lily's arms clamped around her waist, like she'd belonged there all along.

And Lily's voice—bright, unguarded: *Are you gonna be my mommy?* That one dug under my ribs. Still lodged there.

The cursor blinks useless. My ribcage pulls tight. I shut the laptop. Admit what's true: work can wait. This can't.

I cross to Lily, crouch until her eyes meet mine. "Hey, kiddo." My voice carries more weight than I want it to. "How would you feel about spending the afternoon with Patricia?"

Her head pops up, grin flashing. "Can we bake cookies?"

The light in her face loosens something in my chest. I nod. "I think she'd like that."

She squeals, scooping dolls into her arms, already half packed like she's going on vacation.

I watch her spin, socks sliding across wood. Easy. No resistance. My window's clear.

That steadiness roots me. Anchor Lily first. Then Scarlett. One at a time.

The drive over is short, but my mind runs grids anyway. Scarlett. Me. Lily. The baby. Too many variables to lock down a full plan. But I don't need the map yet. Just the first step: show Scarlett she isn't alone.

Patricia meets us at the door. She sweeps Lily in with promises of sugar and crafts. Over her shoulder, Dad nods once at me, steady as always. He doesn't ask questions. Yet.

I press a kiss to Lily's hair. She smells like shampoo and syrup. She waves without looking back, already talking about sprinkles.

Back in the car, the silence is sharp, decisive.

Flowers. Sparkling cider. Dinner in her kitchen. Simple. Not overwhelming. But a signal: presence, intent.

I picture her face when I knock—how she'll hold her breath, how she might brace. And how I'll answer that, steady, no vanishing this time.

By the time I hit the store lot, the plan is set: bouquet in one hand, cider in the other.

Not fate. Choice. Mine.

CHAPTER 17
Flame & Food

Hands brush. Fears name themselves. He doesn't flinch.

SCARLETT

The apartment feels too quiet. The hum of traffic outside, the faint tick of the heater—none of it fills the space.

My phone lies on the coffee table, screen dark, but I keep glancing at it anyway. Yesterday it glowed all day—Eli's consistent check-ins, the picture of him and Lily with shopping bags, both of them grinning. That selfie became my wallpaper before I even thought it through. Now every time I pick up my phone, it's their faces smiling back instead of the cloudscape I'd had for years.

I trace the edge of the phone with my thumb. For hours, his texts anchored me. His tone is so... him. Steady. No exclamation points, no flood of emojis, just presence. *Thinking about Thursday. Glad you came.* A snapshot of Lily's pancake tower, *engineering project, breakfast edition.* A video call so she could say hi, her voice squealing in the background while Eli half-smiled at me from behind the camera.

But now, with the apartment quiet, that old static creeps back in. Did I imagine it? Did it mean the same thing to him? Or was it just a holiday high? My chest tightens. The loop won't stop until I'm with him again.

I've circled the living room so many times the rug corner has curled up. My hands can't stay still—tugging at my sweatshirt hem, brushing my hair back, skimming restless over my stomach. The weight of Lily's words has followed me since Thursday night:

Are you gonna be my mommy? Her arms around my waist, cinnamon pie clinging to her hair. It split me open in ways I can't put back.

The knock lands on the door and everything in me jolts. My stomach dips, breath locking high in my chest. For one suspended beat I just stand there, frozen.

Thanksgiving echoes like a bruise: *I thought you left me.*

My palm presses flat to my stomach, as if I could calm the nerves ricocheting inside.

If it isn't him, the spiral starts again. If it is, then I have to face whatever comes next.

I make myself move. Fingers clumsy on the latch, I pull the door open.

Eli fills the doorway. Wool coat smelling of cold air, bouquet of wildflowers messy and vivid in one hand, sparkling cider catching the light in the other.

Heat rises straight into my cheeks. The bouquet—wild, too bright for November. Not roses, not safe. The kind of choice that feels like he knew me enough to get it right.

The petals brush my skin when I take them. Soft. Real.

"You brought me flowers." My voice betrays more than I want—how much it hits, how much it matters.

He smiles. Warm. Steady. It tilts something loose inside me.

I step back to let him in. His cologne mixes with the green bite of the stems as the door shuts behind him. The cider clinks down on the counter, casual, but it feels like he's anchoring himself here, in my space.

He hefts a canvas grocery bag down next—chicken, garlic, fresh herbs, pasta. Planned. Prepared.

Relief flickers through me, quick as a match. The kitchen is too small for pretense. Space runs out before distance can. Every reach brushes skin, every step pulls him closer, until the air feels heavier than the steam rising from the pan.

My knife wobbles on a garlic clove; the slip is enough for Eli's hand to close over mine, steadying the handle.

Each pass brings him nearer. His sleeve grazes my elbow; my pulse pops in my throat. I swat him with the dish towel, light, a joke that hides more than it shows.

He grins like he sees all the way through it. The tiny kitchen seems to shrink around us, herbs and heat and something heavier thickening the air.

He leans across me for the spice jar; his chest brushes my shoulder, his breath warm at my temple. Then he says my name, low and careful. "Scarlett."

His eyes search mine, a question without sound.

My palm finds his jaw. Answer given. I nod.

The kiss hits hard—all the tension we've been holding splintering at once. My fingers fist tight in his shirt. His hands clamp at my waist and pull me flush; he tastes like warm skin edged with winter air, steady and sure, like the kind of closeness I didn't think I'd ever have again. And the steadiness I've been aching for. The counter digs into my hips. My breathing turns ragged in the space of a heartbeat.

He lifts me like it's nothing, setting me on the cool slab. The contrast jolts; my thighs tighten around him on instinct. When he groans, quiet and wrecked, the sound shoots straight through me. I drag him closer by the hair at his nape, opening for him, drinking the kiss like oxygen.

The skillet's hiss spikes, sharp going bitter.

"Wait—" I break off against his mouth, breath catching. "Garlic."

We lunge shoulder to shoulder. He tilts the pan; I splash broth; steam bursts up, wet and fragrant. The ordinary choreography steadies me—wooden spoon tapping, his forearm brushing mine, my laugh stuttering out as the sharp edge of the garlic burn mellows into something warm and savory again.

When I glance up, he's already watching me with that intent, measuring look. It flips my stomach like a switch.

We plate quickly, scatter parsley, carry everything to the table. For a minute there's only the clink of forks and the kind of quiet that doesn't demand anything.

Then his thumb finds my knuckles under the table, warm and certain, and all the weight I've been holding rushes back to the surface.

"My head keeps splitting in two," I admit, voice barely above a whisper. "Part of me is grateful. The other part is terrified this is moving too fast. That you're only here because of the baby."

He doesn't rush. He sits back a fraction, thinking—really thinking. I can almost hear the gears line up.

"I'm here because of you," he says first, simple and steady. "The baby matters. Of course. But I started searching before I knew. I didn't stop when it would've been easier."

A beat, then his mouth tilts. "If it were just the baby, I'd be responsible. Present. But I wouldn't be here like this—choosing the ordinary with you, wanting to know your weekend moods, your coffee order, why you change your phone wallpaper only for ridiculous selfies. I'm here because with you, the noise in my head gets quiet. And even when it got complicated, I didn't want to step back."

Something unclenches low in my chest. He isn't here out of duty. He's here because of me.

Still, one thread won't let go. "I can still hear her," I whisper. "Lily. *Are you gonna be my mommy?* It's been looping since Thursday. I don't ever want her to feel... replaced."

"She won't." His answer is immediate, sure. "Love expands. It doesn't reassign. We bring her into every decision that touches her. Her pace first." His thumb strokes my hand again. "Your pace, too."

The knot I've been bracing against loosens another click. I didn't realize how hard I was holding it until now.

"When you said that," I murmur, finally lifting my eyes, "it sounded like long haul. All-in."

His gaze holds mine, unwavering. "It is."

We clean up side by side—plates stacked, water running, the small clinks of normal. The rhythm steadies my breathing.

"We should wait until Christmas," I say quietly as I dry the last plate. "Not hiding. Waiting. Choosing the right moment for something this big."

He nods once, no argument, no push. "Christmas," he says. Agreement lands like an anchor.

It hurts, already, to hold something this big. But ache doesn't mean wrong—it means real. And real things deserve the right moment to be named.

Our fingers brush when I pass him the towel. Neither of us moves away.

The lamp throws gold across the living room; the Macintosh candle burns low, apple-sweet. I curl into the corner of the couch, suddenly bone-tired. For a beat I wonder if he'll keep space.

He sits close instead, arm along the back of the couch—an invitation I take without thinking, tucking under his shoulder. His hand slips into my hair, slow, careful. My eyes slide closed on a long exhale.

"I'm still scared," I say into his shirt.

"Good," he murmurs, steady as a vow. "Being scared means it matters. And we can still choose it—us—anyway."

The last echo that lingers isn't Lily's question—it's his answer from the doorway yesterday: *Yes, Lily. This is Scarlett. She's the one.*

The candle burns low. His hand is in my hair, steady, anchoring. I should let the quiet carry us, but the words press sharp against my ribs.

"I need to say something," I whisper. My throat feels raw, but I make myself go on. "I don't... do this. I don't sleep with people I just met. Ever. Not once. You're the only exception."

His eyes steady on mine—no flicker, no mockery. Just calculation, like he's weighing each word. Then his palm shifts, cupping the back of my neck.

"You're the first I've touched in years," he says simply. "I don't risk chaos. Not with my life. Not with Lily's. Not with you."

Something loosens in me, slow and quiet. He didn't need to say it, but he did. And I believe him.

And with his hand warm in my hair, I fall asleep.

CHAPTER 18
Lights & Letters

Holiday crowd. Careful hands. Two initials on a tree.

ELI

The house is quiet; the heater breathes. I'm up before Lily, coffee cooling on the counter, the phone face-down beside it so I don't stare like a teenager. A week of workdays wedged between us and Thanksgiving has stretched longer than it should; we didn't push for overnights, didn't rush anything. We texted; we Face-Timed. I learned the cadence of her evenings—tea at nine, the way she tucks her hair when she's thinking, how she smiles without showing teeth when she's tired. I learned which prenatal vitamins she bought and that they live on her kitchen shelf, not mine. I set a reminder anyway: take with food, don't forget B6 for nausea. Not control—support. Structure so she doesn't have to remember everything herself.

The phone buzzes. A small, ordinary jolt.

I flip it, grin breaking before I tell it not to.

> **Awake. Pancakes are happening.**

Pancakes—good. She hasn't been able to keep break-fast down. That means today is better. It also decides mine. I'll make them for Lily.

Another buzz.

> **I keep glancing at my phone like a raccoon digging through bins.**

I huff. It's her shorthand—restless, scavenging for re-assurance she hasn't missed my texts. That's her trans-lation. I get it.

> I'm here. 11 a.m. pickup still good?

Yes. Layers x 100?

> Layers. Water. Snacks. No heroics.

Bossy.

> Prepared.

Fine. Prepared is hot.

Her words hit with precision. I've spent years carrying duty like armor, convinced it read as rigidity. She calls it strength. Wantable. That recalibrates something in me. I've been holding the question back, waiting for the right place to ask, but maybe this is the place—proof she doesn't think I'm intruding.

> Do you want me there Wednesday?

Yes.

> Done. I'll take the morning.

"Daddy?" Lily's voice lands at my elbow. She's a tangle of pajamas, hair sleep-warm, eyes bright.

"Hi, kiddo." I scoop her up for a second, memorize the weight I know will shift again by spring. "Holiday market after lunch. Then the tree."

"And Scarlett?" she asks. Direct, like she asks about a new book at school.

"And Scarlett," I say. Her smile answers something I didn't say out loud.

We run the morning on rails: pancakes, a hunt for Lily's right boot, the mittens we lost and mysteriously find under the couch. On the drive, the city looks rinsed clean, sunlight cold and bright, the kind that makes everything look outlined. Lily hums a mash-up of carols from the back seat, and I try not to check the time every two blocks.

Scarlett's waiting at the curb in a slate coat and a knit hat with a ridiculous pom-pom that somehow doesn't look ridiculous on *her*. She's flushed from the cold, and when she sees us, the worry line between her brows smooths like a hand pressed over it. Lily waves hard enough to nearly dislocate something. I'm out and around before the car fully stops, because I'm not going to let Scarlett stand there juggling a tote bag and a thermos while I sit behind glass.

"Hi," she says, soft, the shy of it not uncertainty so much as recalibration: public, day, Lily in the back, my world around us. She slides in and turns immediately, "Hi, Lily," and Lily announces that there will be cookies later and Scarlett says that is top tier cookie logic.

The air smells of cinnamon, roasted chestnuts, kettle corn, and a faint curl of woodsmoke from the fire pits at the edge of the square. Stalls string lights like constellations, and a brass quartet does its damndest with "O Holy Night." Lily threads herself between us, gloved hands in both of ours when the crowd presses. I keep a scanning eye open—stroller wheels, a dog on the wrong side of a leash, a teen dragging a sled at shin height—but mostly I watch Scarlett's shoulders ease down notch by notch. She fits here. Not as anyone else I thought she might be. As her.

We stop at a booth with ornaments made from old typewriter keys. Lily finds one with an L. Scarlett fingers a small silver S and then sets it back, like buying it would say too much too soon. I buy it anyway, tuck it into my pocket beside the L Lily found earlier, and don't hand either over yet.

Hot chocolate comes next—Lily with extra marshmallows, me with none, Scarlett halfway between. She blows across the surface and closes her eyes at the

first sip like warmth travelled straight to her bones.
When we move again, she stays tucked under my arm
without thinking. That muscle in my chest that only
relaxes when things are where they should be—relaxes.

By the time we make it to the tree lot, the sun's shifted, gilding everything it touches. The air has that edge
that stings your lungs in the first breath, then goes
unnoticed as your body adjusts.

Rows of firs and spruces stand like a tiny disciplined
forest. Lily bolts to a gigantic one and hugs it; I crouch
and explain ceilings, math, and the difference between
"cozy" and "sleeping in a forest."

Scarlett kneels to tie tags once we choose, her gloves
clumsy, her laugh catching on the plastic threading.
She hands the little tag to Lily like it's a formal job. It
is.

Sawing is ritual. Lily's hand on the handle, my hand
over hers. "Slow. Let the saw do the work," I say, and
she repeats it under her breath like spellwork. Scarlett leans close but stays clear of the arc. The trunk
gives with a soft crack; Lily cheers; I do the boring
parts—blanket on the roof, straps crossed, knots set,
tug twice.

Scarlett watches the second tug and makes fun of me. I shrug. "I like keeping the windshield intact," I say. She grins, teeth finally showing.

Scarlett's phone buzzes. She glances down, lips curving faintly. "Mom says—gingerbread assembly next Sunday."

I catch her eye over the roof of the car. "We'll go."

Her smile lifts easier this time. "Yeah. We'll go."

Back at my place, the living room turns constructive chaos: boxes opened, tissue paper everywhere, cocoa on the stove because the cocoa must always be on the stove in December.

Lily goes wrist-deep into the ornament bin, glitter adhering to her like static. I test the lights strand by strand. Scarlett takes the spot beside me on the arm of the couch, hip a warm line against my shoulder. I'm aware of the weight of every inch she rests on me and how easily I could forget to move.

"Classic red and green?" she asks, tone that says she's ready to tease me.

"Classic," I confirm, "reliable." Then let my mouth tilt. "Or maybe vintage."

She hums low, amused. "Vintage and reliable—that's you. Looks good on you, too."

Heat sparks in my chest, but I keep it contained, pulling her in for a quick kiss and letting it be exactly that—quick. Boundaries aren't punishment. They're what lets us build steady.

"Daddy!" Lily calls. "Put the glitter heart in the front." She holds up the ornament we made last weekend, glue still thick where her name skidded.

Scarlett kneels, eye level. "Front and center," she decrees, and Lily straightens like she just earned a medal.

I put it where they tell me, then climb the step stool for the star. Lily argues for a tilt; I give her half of what she wants, because compromise is a lesson, and she beams like I conceded a galaxy.

While they're fussing over placement, I slip my hand into the ornament box. The little **L** I picked up at the market glints in the tissue paper where I tucked it earlier. Lily dives in a second later and gasps when she finds it. "This one's me!" she crows, holding the typewriter key high.

Scarlett blinks when I pull the **S** from my pocket. Her fingers hover before I hook it beside Lily's, brushing her hand as I do.

Her smile curves soft, unsteady, like it's bigger than she knows how to hold.

Two letters catching the lights, side by side. My girls, claimed by the tree.

Later, we walk the neighborhood loop to burn cocoa energy and watch windows bloom with trees. Lily narrates which houses have the "right" lights (white) and which are "grumpy" (blue). Scarlett listens like every opinion is real data. When we're home again, I make grilled cheeses that would make a cardiologist frown.

Scarlett settles on the couch with Lily, reading one of the Christmas books Patricia dropped off. Lily leans against her side, rapt at every page turn, voice piping up to guess the rhymes before Scarlett gets there. I watch from the kitchen as I rinse plates, every sound of Scarlett's voice carrying clear.

When it's time to drive her home, Lily stages a small protest, wrapping herself around Scarlett's waist like an octopus. Scarlett laughs, gently peels her loose, then kneels to promise, "Next Sunday—gingerbread at Grandpa Richard's. Scout's honor," she says solemnly, and Lily checks, "Were you a Scout?" Scarlett admits she was not, but she respects the concept, and Lily deems this acceptable.

Mrs. Green from next door steps in to keep Lily company for the half-hour round trip; she's done it before, and Lily barely notices, too busy setting out pajamas for bedtime.

At her building, the street is quiet enough to hear the faraway train. I walk her to the door because of course I do. The night hangs cold and clear; our breaths show and vanish.

We stand there a beat too long, all the practical words already spoken in the car—
text me when you're inside; Wednesday works for the appointment; I'll take the morning for it; bring snacks; you'll remind me to breathe; I'll remind you to eat something first.

"I'm glad today was today," she says, fingers slipping into my coat sleeve, not quite taking my hand, just claiming the space around it.

"Me too." My voice sounds lower in winter air. "You okay?"

She nods. The nod has weight. "I am." A pause. "It helps that you... think of the things before I have to."

"That's my job," I say. "It was before. It is now."

"Not just Lily," she says, and the way she says it lands somewhere I don't let many things land.

We keep the kiss at the door contained—heat, yes, but measured, held at our lips and nowhere further. Her hand slips against the side of my neck; my palm spreads over the curve of her hip through the fabric of her coat; both of us breathe in like we forgot how.

"Text me when you're up there," I say. "And take the vitamins with real food, not just tea."

"Yes, sir." The tease takes the edge off the part where I hate not walking her all the way to the stairwell and also know I shouldn't.

I watch until she's inside, wait for the buzz on my phone.

> Inside. I still smell the Christmas tree.

Then I drive home with the heat up one notch higher than usual.

Back at the house, I do the small resets: mugs in the sink to soak, cocoa pot filled with water, lights on the tree set to a slow breath instead of a blink.

Lily is a sprawl in her bed, mouth open, stuffed reindeer half-fallen beside her. I tuck it closer to her arm so it won't hit the floor, then step back.

In the quiet, I pull out my phone and open the calendar. Wednesday, 10:40 a.m.—OB intake. I block the time and two hours around it—because delays happen, because waiting rooms swallow time whole. I add a note: B6 lozenges; granola in glove box; water bottle.

The heater exhales. The lights on the tree rise and fall like sleep. I think about odds again—not fate, not magic—just improbable variables that lined up: wrong costume, right woman, a month of missed connections, a door opening in a house that smells like cinnamon and kid shampoo and fresh-cut fir. The math doesn't care about meaning. I do.

My phone buzzes once more.

> Thanks for today. For planning it, but also for letting it just… be.

> My pleasure. Sleep.

> Working on it. Goodnight.

> Goodnight.

I set the phone face down, not because I want to ignore it, but because we both need the space. I double-check the thermostat. I turn off the lamp. I stand at the doorway of Lily's room and listen to her breathe, and then I lie down in my own bed and picture Wednesday morning—her hand in mine under fluorescent lights, the sound of a new heartbeat threading its way through the static.

A thing that did not exist on any of my spreadsheets a month ago and now is the axis my days tilt around.

CHAPTER 19

Proof & Pulse

One flicker on a screen changes everything.

SCARLETT

The waiting room hums with low noise—the buzz of overhead lights, the glare of muted cartoons, magazines fanned across the tables. I sit too straight in the plastic chair, palms damp against my thighs. Eli's hand folds around mine, thumb brushing slow across my knuckles like he's smoothing out static.

"You're shaking a little," he says quietly.

I force a breath. "I'm fine."

His eyes catch mine, steady, unblinking. He doesn't call me out. Just keeps my fingers laced with his, an anchor until the nurse calls my name.

The exam is a blur—blood pressure, paperwork, questions I answer with a dry mouth. But when the ultrasound wand presses cool against my skin and the screen blinks to life, the room tilts. A pulse. A flicker. Something impossibly small, impossibly real.

My throat tightens. Tears prick fast.

Eli's grip on my hand sharpens. I glance sideways, and his jaw is taut, his eyes locked on the screen like he's memorizing every pixel. "That's ours." His voice roughens, no space for doubt.

I can only nod, tears slipping free.

By the time we step back into the chill daylight, my head is spinning. The folder of printouts feels heavy in my hands. Eli takes it without asking, tucks it neatly under his arm.

In the car, silence stretches—not empty, but weighted with everything we just saw. He drives one-handed, the other covering mine on the console. No words. Just presence.

At my building, I hesitate, hand on the door. He studies me, reading what I can't say.

"Tea?" I ask, needing him to stay, even just a little longer.

Something sparks in his eyes—relief, maybe, or restraint cracking just enough. "Tea," he agrees.

Inside, I fuss with the kettle, too aware of him leaning against the counter, coat still on, eyes tracking me. The quiet grows heavier. When I reach for mugs, he steps in close, reaching over my shoulder for the sugar tin. His chest brushes my back, his breath warm against my hairline.

The world narrows. My pulse hammers. I turn, and suddenly his mouth is on mine.

The kiss is rougher than the kitchen last week, hungrier, like every second apart tightened this coil until now. My hands fist in his shirt; his palm finds my hip, pulling me hard against him. The counter presses into my spine as heat spirals sharp and dizzy.

I gasp into him, and he swallows the sound, deepening the kiss. For one suspended moment, I let myself drown in it—his taste, his steadiness, the sheer inevitability of us.

Then his phone buzzes. Loud. Insistent.

He freezes, forehead dropping to mine with a groan. "Damn it."

The calendar reminder flares on his screen. He silences it, jaw flexing. "Work. I have to go."

His eyes flick over me, still caught in the residue of the kiss. "Friday. Dinner at my place?"

My pulse kicks. I nod. "Yes."

He kisses me again—slower this time, deliberate, like he's sealing a promise. When he pulls back, his voice is low, rough. "Next time, Scarlett. I'm not stopping at a kiss."

CHAPTER 20
Cider & Intent

He sets the scene. You say yes with your whole body.

SCARLETT

Friday evening, the air sharp with December cold. I open the door and Eli is there—dark coat, collar turned up, the quiet steadiness in his eyes cutting right through the bite of wind that trails in with him.

He doesn't say much, just holds my coat out for me. His fingers graze mine as I push my arms through, a brush so small it still jolts. When he settles the collar against my neck, his touch lingers, his gaze catching on the lace panel at the back of my dress. A flicker of heat, quickly banked, but not missed.

We don't head to dinner. Not yet. Instead, he drives us into the heart of downtown. The square glows like a snow globe shaken to life—strings of gold and silver lights crisscrossing the streets, wreaths hanging from lampposts, shop windows layered in garlands and ribbon. The air smells like pine and cinnamon, carried from vendor stalls. Families guide bundled children past us; couples tuck close against the cold.

Eli threads us into the crowd without hesitation. He doesn't hide. His hand finds mine—casual, firm. Not avoiding. Choosing. My chest stumbles at the simplicity of it. The smallness of that gesture cracks something open in me.

We stop at a cart steaming with hot drinks. He orders black coffee for himself, cider for me. When he passes it over, our fingers brush, and my heart jolts.

"You're staring," I say, trying for playful, but my voice wobbles.

"Memorizing," he answers, flat and certain. No smile, no flinch—just fact. It lands deeper than flattery, as if he's already keeping a record of me.

We walk beneath archways of white lights that drip from the buildings like stars made tangible. My boots crunch against frost; his stride steadying my pace. Every step, every graze of his shoulder against me, winds the tension tighter.

Then we stop. The canopy overhead glitters, flooding the square with a false daylight. He bends slightly, eyes never leaving mine. I tip up to meet him, and when our mouths touch, the world compresses to that single point of contact.

The kiss is soft at first—lingering, steady. But beneath it runs the charge of everything unsaid. His thumb strokes once across the back of my hand before we part, deliberate, grounding.

I draw in a breath that feels too big for my lungs. I already know—my chest too tight, my skin too live—this night doesn't end here.

CHAPTER 21

Lace & Limits

Every move is patient—until it isn't.

ELI

I plan it. Not elaborate—intentional. After downtown, we don't go to a restaurant. We come here.

The tree glows in the corner. Candles flicker on the table, the kind that shut off with a switch so I don't risk smoke. Dinner waits in the oven on low, the fire steady, music low enough that silence can sit between notes. Every variable accounted for.

Scarlett deserves intention.

The table is already set when we step inside. Plates warmed in the oven. Bread resting under a towel so the crust stays right. Her eyes sweep the room, then soften, warm enough to undo me.

Scarlett steps into the light, black dress clinging smooth to her frame. Boots to her knees, zipper line tempting in its precision. I take her coat slow, not because I have to but because I want the extra seconds to look. When the fabric slips free, the lace panel at the back is revealed—fine as wiring traced by hand, almost transparent up close. My fingers itch to test its texture. I don't. Not yet.

"You did all this?"

"Yes." Nothing more is needed.

"Sparkling cider or water?" I ask, already setting the bottle down.

"Cider," she says, soft.

I pour, the fizz climbing the glass. When I slide it to her, my knuckle grazes the inside of her wrist. Not accident. Data point. Her pulse beats fast there. She doesn't move away.

We sit. Plates uncovered: roast chicken, rosemary potatoes, green beans snapped that morning. Not extravagant, but intentional.

She starts talking—work deadlines, Tessa's ridiculous tree—pink tinsel, apparently—the way the office is pretending productivity this close to Christmas. I listen. Really listen. Every word catalogued. Every inflection a thread I want to pull.

Her hand drifts to her glass. Mine follows with the bottle, refill not needed. Fingers overlap. Her breath catches—subtle, but I file it.

I pass the bread. Our palms brush, slow enough to register. I tuck a loose strand of her hair behind her ear, and the back of my knuckle trails her collarbone. Warm skin. She swallows. Another data point.

I don't crowd her. Every move is incremental. A wrist graze here. A palm settling over hers when I hand the knife. *Contact → pause → watch → confirm.* She's not pulling away. She's leaning in, even when she pretends she's focused on her plate.

By the time dessert would normally appear, the food has cooled and we haven't touched half of it. Not because the meal failed. Because the calibration succeeded.

Restraint is my specialty. Tonight, it frays.

I push back from the table, stand, and hold out my hand. "Come."

Her fingers slide into mine, warm and deliberate. I lead her to the couch. Not rushed. Not casual. Chosen.

I kneel on the rug, both knees grounding me. Her breath stutters like she feels the shift in gravity. I catch the first zipper, the rasp of metal teeth loud in the hush. My knuckles brush bare skin above the leather, and she gasps. Not protest. Confirmation.

I ease the boot free, press my mouth once to the inside of her knee—light, testing. She exhales sharp, hand twitching against the cushion. Green light.

The second boot. Same ritual. Zipper sliding down. My lips find her higher this time, at the soft slope above her knee. Her thighs tighten, then relax, and her pupils blow wide. Anticipation, not retreat.

Both boots set neatly beside the couch, order preserved. But there's nothing orderly left in me. My palms rest just above her knees, heat bleeding through fabric. I lift my eyes. "Remember what I told you?" My voice comes rougher than I intend. "Next time. It's next time."

Color rises in her throat. She nods. Her hand slips into my hair, fingers curling. Signal undeniable.

I rise slowly, one hand steady on her hip, the other braced on the couch. When I kiss her, it isn't rushed—it's deliberate, mapped. Her mouth opens under mine, hungry, unguarded. She fists my shirt, pulling me closer.

Fabric turns obstacle. I push her dress higher, fingers brushing lace. Her body arches, breath breaking. She's giving me everything. I adjust angle, deepen the kiss, until she melts back into the cushions.

I reach for my wallet—habit, non-negotiable. The foil slides free, tears soft in my hand.

Her palm closes over mine. Small. Certain. "Eli." Her voice is low, unsteady but clear. "I'm already pregnant."

The words land hot under my ribs—trust offered without armor. I shake my head once. "This isn't about that. It's respect. Safety. No variables left loose."

Her eyes soften like I've undone her more with those words than any kiss. She nods, breathless, gaze steady. Waiting.

When I press into her, it's slow, deliberate. She gasps into my mouth, sharp and helpless. Perfect fit. The rhythm locks quick, inevitable as gravity. Her hands clutch at my back, legs hooking around me, pulling me deeper.

I read every cue. The tremor when I angle lower. The catch in her breath when I draw back slow, then drive harder. Nails scrape my skin; her head tips back, voice breaking raw.

"Again," I murmur against her ear. Her body tightens, release breaking through her. I hold to her rhythm, then follow when she pulls me under, pulse unraveling into hers.

We collapse together, breath harsh, muscles buzzing. Her laugh is shaky, wrecked, perfect. She teases me about dessert gone cold. I promise restitution, and her laugh curls into me like reward.

Candlelight flickers across her face, hair spilling over my arm, lips swollen from my mouth. The ache in my chest isn't just desire—it's resolve.

The calculation's already run. The outcome's fixed: I won't let her go.

CHAPTER 22

Patterns & Peace

It's not chance. It's proof. Breathe.

SCARLETT

By the time I'm back in my apartment, everything looks the same—mail slumped by the door, the crooked frame on the wall, the candle burned down to wick.

But I don't feel the same.

I can still feel him—the slow drag of a zipper loosening leather, his mouth at my knee, the way his hand steadied my hip like he had nowhere else to be. He read me with patience, every touch chosen. That changed everything.

My body hums with it still. Not sore—awake. Sensitive in ways I didn't know I could be. Marked, but not possessed. His presence lingers like heat in my skin, invisible but undeniable.

The boots I kicked off sit by the door. On the counter, the orange bottle of prenatal vitamins catches the light. I pause, twist it open, swallow one with tap water. Bitter on my tongue, steadying in my chest. A reminder: this isn't just romance. It's responsibility. My body isn't only mine anymore.

Still, the loop starts: Too fast. Too much. What if it was only heat? What if I misread him? What if he wakes up different? The what-ifs press tight against my ribs.

I curl on the couch with a blanket, phone in my lap, trying to breathe steady.

The buzz startles me.

> Thinking about you. Glad last night wasn't chance. It's pattern.

Of course he'd phrase it like that. Still, my chest loosens. My thumbs move before I can overthink.

> Pattern? You make it sound like a math problem.

> Not math. Proof. Every variable points to the same answer: us.

I bite my lip, eyes stinging.

> You sound so sure.

> Because you chose me back. You didn't have to. That matters more than anything else.

The words settle like warmth in my chest.

> You make it sound simple.

> It is. Complicated things can still be steady. You, me, Lily, the baby—we're steady now.

My throat burns. I press the phone to my chest, feeling my heartbeat thrum against the screen. For the first time all day, the loop eases.

...You always know how to shut up the noise in my head.

Good. That's the job I want.

The phone dims. Quiet rushes back in. But it doesn't feel heavy this time.

I curl deeper into the couch, hand brushing over my stomach. Fear flickers, but hope roots deeper.

Pattern. Proof. Together.

Tomorrow is gingerbread at Mom's. After that—Christmas.

CHAPTER 23
Gumdrops & Guilt

Family warmth. A secret that won't sit still.

SCARLETT

Richard's kitchen smells like gingerbread and sugar before we've even shed our coats. The table is already staged for chaos—parchment spread out, bowls of gumdrops and peppermints glittering under the overhead light, icing bags sagging in a row like tools waiting for their turn.

"Okay, architects," Mom announces, clapping her hands. "Your materials await."

Lily bounces on her toes, mittens still dangling from her sleeves. "We're gonna win!" she crows, even though there's no contest, just family.

Eli crouches to help her peel off her coat, steady hands tugging zippers, smoothing flyaway hair. He doesn't glance at me, but the corner of his mouth tips like he feels me watching. Like he remembers Friday night too. Heat pricks low in my chest.

I slide into a chair beside Lily. She leans close, conspiratorial, and presses a marshmallow into my palm like it's a secret pact. "We can eat some too," she whispers, eyes wide.

Her joy cracks me open. I grin back. "Only if we don't tell the building inspector."

She giggles, high and bright, loud enough to draw Eli's attention. His eyes meet mine across the candy bowls. For a beat, gumdrops blur. Lace. Heat. His mouth at my throat—Friday surging back so fast my cheeks flame. I look down fast, fingers sticky with sugar.

Richard sets coffee on the counter, sleeves rolled to his elbows. He's not Eli—softer jaw, quicker laugh—but I see where Eli's steadiness comes from. The way Richard fits next to Mom—her energy, his calm—makes something twist inside me. I judged her for moving fast. And yet, look. They work.

We start building. Icing thick as mortar, walls balanced against teetering roofs. Lily presses too hard, one side buckles. "It's falling!" she yelps.

"Structural support coming in," Eli says, slipping in behind her chair. His hand braces the wall, guiding Lily's smaller one. His arm brushes mine as I lean in to steady the roof. Heat jolts through me, the remembered charge of moving in sync with him. Together we hold until it sets.

Richard nods like a judge passing sentence. "Structural integrity restored."

Mom claps, eyes shining. "Look at that teamwork." She slips a candy cane into Lily's hand and then another into mine, like she can't help rewarding everyone at once. Her warmth folds over me, uninvited but impossible not to lean into. Guilt prickles sharp under it. She doesn't even know.

"Scarlett?" Mom's voice gentles. "Want to help with the frosting flowers?"

I make myself smile. "Of course."

The piping bag is slick with sugar. My fingers tighten too much; icing squirts in a messy star. Eli reaches for the red candies, arm brushing mine again. Not accident. Not neutral. My breath catches, and he steadies the bag with one hand, his thumb brushing mine just long enough to ground me. The contact lingers—too much for family eyes, but I can't make myself pull away.

By the time we're done, the house leans left, gumdrops crooked, frosting slipping like thawed snow. Lily claps her hands, sticky fingers leaving prints on my sleeve. "We made it together!"

The words lands sweet and sharp all at once. My throat burns, but I pull her into my lap, brushing the sugar from her hairline.

Mom snaps a photo, fussing with the angle. Richard holds the lamp so the gumdrops sparkle. Eli catches my eye over Lily's head, and heat sparks again. His mouth curves—barely—but it's enough to tighten everything in me.

We linger too long, sugar crusting on our fingers, coffee cooling in mugs. Lily insists on carrying the crooked house to the living room mantle, and Mom humors her, clearing a space like it's a masterpiece. Richard helps with coats, ruffling Lily's hair as he passes. She tilts her head into his hand without thinking, instinctive as breathing.

Mom slips my scarf around my neck, tucking the ends like she used to when I was little. Her warmth makes my throat tighten. She doesn't even know she's about to be a grandmother, and here she is, loving me like she already sees the whole picture.

"You'll come by again before Christmas?" she asks, her hand lingering on my arm.

I swallow. "Of course." The promise is true, but incomplete—the part I can't give her yet lodges sharp in my throat.

Eli steps in, coat collar turned up, Lily's mittened hand tight in his. His eyes flick to mine, steady, reading everything I can't say out loud. The silent agreement between us—Christmas—is still there. Still right. But guilt buzzes in my chest as we say goodnight.

Outside, the cold slams harder after all that warmth. Eli opens the car door, his hand warm at my back as I duck in. Lily chatters about gumdrops from the back seat, voice bright, sticky-sweet.

I press my forehead to the glass, breath fogging, porch lights smearing into glow. Eli's fingers find mine on the console, steady. Friday still hums in my skin, but tonight's secret presses tighter under my ribs.

Just hold until Christmas.

CHAPTER 24
Cinnamon & Certainty

Calm morning. Ready the reveal.

ELI

Christmas morning runs on rails: Lily thunders down the hall before the sun's fully up, shrieking about stockings, hair tangled in every direction. Scarlett follows slower, robe pulled tight, eyes still soft with sleep. She smiles when Lily dumps a pile of wrapping paper in her lap, but there's a knot at the edges—nerves coiled under the warmth.

I keep the rhythm steady: coffee poured, cinnamon rolls on plates, the small gifts we kept here unwrapped with a deliberate pace so nothing feels rushed. Lily squeals over a science kit. Scarlett unwraps a bright box of markers and watercolor paper, the kind any kid would gravitate toward in a store. Her laugh spills free, light and unguarded.

"So you can draw with me," Lily explains solemnly, and Scarlett hugs her like it's the best thing she's ever been given.

The sound is real, but Scarlett keeps glancing at the tree, then at me, as if bracing for what comes next.

She doesn't say it, but I know. Holding the secret has scraped her raw. Today she finally gets to set it down.

I've already gamed out the odds. Ninety-nine percent says the family will celebrate. One percent says someone frowns, freezes, questions timing. I have contingencies for both—words rehearsed, exits mapped, the fallback of waiting until the room is smaller. But I don't think we'll need them.

What I do know is this: once it's spoken, she'll breathe easier. And if she steadies, Lily steadies. That's the axis everything else turns on.

By midmorning, the car is loaded with gifts and Lily's still in her new pajamas. Scarlett sits quiet beside me, her hand in mine, her thumb brushing once against my knuckle, a signal without words.

"Yes," I tell her, even though she hasn't asked it out loud. "We've got this."

By the time Dad and Patricia's house comes into view, the porch light glowing against the frost, her shoulders have eased a fraction. It's enough.

CHAPTER 25
Ribbon & Relief

Two words: Best Big Sister. Belonging lands.

SCARLETT

Christmas morning at Mom and Richard's feels like stepping inside a snow globe—tree lights glowing, gingerbread in the air, carols threading soft through the living room. Lily and her cousins tear into gifts on the rug, their laughter like bells. I sit on the couch beside Eli, our hands brushing, my heart thrumming with nerves.

He leans close, his voice low, private. "You ready?" His thumb strokes my knuckles, steady, anchoring.

I nod, though my pulse is a rabbit in my throat. For weeks, we've carried this secret. Today, we tell them.

The chatter around us ebbs as Eli stands, pulling me up with him. Every gaze turns toward us—their curiosity like heat on my skin. I swallow, bracing.

"We have one more gift," Eli says, his tone calm but edged with emotion. "This year, Scarlett and I have a surprise to share."

He kneels in front of Lily, and I follow, resting a hand on his shoulder for courage. He reaches behind the tree and produces a box tied with red ribbon.

"This one's for you, sweetheart," he tells her.

Lily's eyes shine as she unties the ribbon and lifts the lid. Inside, folded small, is a tiny white t-shirt. She holds it up, her voice quivering with wonder as she reads the letters aloud: "Best Big Sister."

The room goes still. Even the fire seems to hold its breath.

"I'm... going to be a big sister?" Lily whispers, the words wobbling between shock and wonder.

Eli pulls her into a hug. "Yes, you are. The best big sister ever."

The words ripple outward. Mom gasps, her hand flying to her mouth. Sam's eyes go wide. Richard leans forward, brows rising. For a heartbeat, no one speaks.

Then the room erupts. Mom is on her feet first, sweeping me into her arms with tears spilling down her cheeks. "Oh, sweetheart! This is wonderful news!" Her voice cracks, and for once, I let myself sink into her embrace like a daughter instead of a guest.

Richard claps Eli on the back, his grin warm. "Congratulations, son. This is the best gift we could've asked for."

Sam, of course, can't help herself. She squeezes me tight, then leans back, smirking through her tears. "Well, that explains the glow. Let me guess—Halloween? So what, about ten weeks?"

Laughter ripples around the room. My cheeks flush, but Eli's hand steadies at my waist, grounding me.

Lily beams, hugging the shirt to her chest like it's treasure. "I'm wearing this all day," she declares, tugging it over her pajamas then and there. The sight makes my throat tighten. She isn't worried or afraid. She's proud.

The rest of the morning blurs with hugs, toasts of cider, and talk of names and nurseries. I catch Eli's gaze across the room once, and his expression says what words can't: We did it. We're not alone in this.

His hand covers mine, warm and certain. For the first time, the weight in my chest lifts. Not a secret. Not a risk. A beginning.

CHAPTER 26

Boxes & Beginnings

You leave the old. You walk into home.

SCARLETT

I take one last look around the apartment Tessa and I have shared since graduation—our first real place as adults. The cabinet still squeaks, the window still rattles with every bus, the coffee table still bears its circle of mug rings. The laughter, the tears, the late-night movie marathons—they're pressed into the walls. It looks the same, but the air feels different—like it already knows I'm leaving.

Tessa tapes the last box shut, the sound sharp in the quiet. She glances at me, emotion glinting through her smile. "You ready?"

I nod, lump in my throat. "Yeah. But this doesn't mean you're rid of me. Girl nights are still happening."

"You better," she says, watery laugh. "I've got a niece or nephew coming—I'm gonna be their favorite human, no contest."

Her words steady me. "I know you will."

The door creaks. Eli steps in with the cold on his shoulders, Mark and Dad behind him for the heavy lifting. Eli wraps an arm around me. "You okay?"

I lean in. "Yeah. It's a lot. But I'm ready."

Tessa wipes her eyes and points a finger at him. "Take care of her, Carrington. Or I'll hunt you down."

He just dips his chin, solemn. "Always."

The day becomes motion: boxes down the stairs, our breath puffing white in the cold, the dolly clattering against concrete. At the van, I pause with the final box. Behind me, the half-empty living room. Ahead, a whole new life: Eli, Lily, our baby, a home. Bittersweet, but excitement rises under it.

Tessa and I hug at the curb, too long, neither wanting to be first to let go. When we do, our smiles are real. "Don't be a stranger," she says thickly.

"I'll be back so much you'll get sick of me."

"Impossible." She waves from the stoop in her ridiculous cat slippers until we turn the corner.

The drive feels like a page flip—bare trees, winter sky, snow dusting the roads. My thoughts drift to Lily: missing socks, glitter glue disasters, bedtime stories that stretch too long. I want all of it.

And then—there she is. Her face smashes against the front window, then she explodes onto the porch, ponytail flying. The door bursts open and she rockets out, boots thudding. "Scarlett! You're here!"

"I am. And guess what? I brought all my stuff."

She latches onto a box labeled *SCARLETT'S BOOKS*, wobbling under the weight but determined.

"This one's heavy. But I'm strong!" she huffs, until Eli smoothly swaps it for a lighter one marked *SCARVES*.

She beams, hugging it like treasure. "I can carry this one all by myself."

"Perfect," I say, smiling. "Lead the way."

Inside, the smell of cocoa and cookies wraps warm around me. Across the entryway hangs a crooked banner in glitter marker: *WELCOME HOME SCARLETT.* Lily bounces on her toes under it. "Patricia helped me make it!"

Mom steps forward with a mug between her hands, her smile soft and certain. "Welcome home, sweetheart."

My throat tightens. I take the mug, but it's her arms I fold into for a second longer than planned. "Thanks, Mom." The word feels right in my mouth in a way it hasn't for years—like it's been waiting for this moment to mean what it should.

Over my shoulder, Richard is already hauling a box up the stairs with Mark behind him, their laughter mixing with Sam corralling the boys. The whole house hums with motion, but in this moment, it's just me and Mom, and the look in her eyes says she knows exactly how big this step is.

By dusk, boxes are broken down by the back door, the rooms already lived in. Lily is out cold mid-sentence, Eli's Henley is tossed over a chair, my mug is in the "special cabinet." I sink onto the couch, muscles aching, heart steady.

Eli nudges me, eyes warm. "Packed, moved, and unpacked in one day. That's efficiency."

"That's what happens when you let me make the lists."

His mouth tips. "Then keep making them."

The cushion dips, and a second later his chest is at my back, his breath warm against my ear. His arm slides low around my waist, sure, claiming space that already feels like ours.

My fingers trace his jaw.

He kisses my temple. "Welcome home, Scarlett."

The words land like a frame finally leveled. My chest loosens; breath snags. This is it—our beginning.

But beginnings are fragile. I know how quickly life can tilt. And as I rest my head against his shoulder, the fire crackling low, snow ticking at the window—one thought threads steady through my chest: hold on tight.

CHAPTER 27
Systems & Shifts

The creamer moves. The heart doesn't.

ELI

The first week of living together taught me this: falling asleep with Scarlett was easy. Living with her was the adjustment.

Not the big things—we agreed on bills, Lily's routines, how to spend evenings. It was the small things. The ones no one warns you about.

The refrigerator, for instance. Scarlett tucked her oat creamer into the door. Logical. Accessible. Except the door was already part of a system—condiments stacked by height, drinks nested tight, nothing wasted. Her creamer broke the sequence. I moved it back. She moved it out. Every time.

One morning she caught me in the act.

"You moved it again." Eyebrows arched.

"It fits the system here." My tone sharper than I meant.

Her lips pressed together—quiet tell. "I put it in the door because I don't want to move everything around, Eli."

We didn't argue. But the silence afterward carried more weight than I liked.

Later, cooking dinner together, she measured spices with that meticulous calm that makes me want to stand and watch. I reached for the pan. "If you sauté the garlic first, the flavor compounds—"

She cut me a look. "I know. That's why it's step three in the recipe I'm literally reading."

I meant it as help. She heard condescension. The air thinned, sharp enough to sting. Ten minutes later she wanted me to taste-test the sauce, leaning against my shoulder, eager for my input—when she asked for it. And the way her hip pressed lightly into mine as I leaned in—unintentional, but undeniable—short-circuited my irritation. Heat pulsed low, reminder that even our arguments carried their own gravity. Still, the inconsistency had my brain chasing rules that kept shifting.

The pizza sealed it. I ordered pineapple-and-ham—her favorite—but they were out of thick crust, so I got thin. Logical substitution.

She pushed it away. "I don't like pineapple on thin crust. Only thick."

Frustration cut through before I could stop it. "Then what do you want me to do, Scarlett? Read your mind?"

Her face fell. Instantly I regretted it. Because in her head the alternative was obvious: mushroom and olive on thin. Perfectly consistent to her logic. Completely invisible to mine.

That night, after Lily was asleep, I found Scarlett curled on the couch, book open on her chest, blanket sliding off her shoulder. Her hand rested light on her stomach even in sleep, protective.

I bent to adjust the blanket. Irritation drained. The fridge, the garlic, the pizza—they didn't matter. What mattered was this: she was here. She'd chosen here.

For years, this house had been efficient. Ordered. Mine. Now it wasn't just my system anymore. She moved things, made calls, left traces of herself in the space. Not disorder—just not only mine. And the shift was permanent. And better.

I sat back and let the fire crackle. Her steady breathing filled the room.

For once, staying was the plan. Still, I mapped what-ifs in the margins. Order isn't weakness; it's how I keep them safe. And now that I have them, safety isn't optional.

CHAPTER 28

Frost & Forever

Love isn't borrowed. It's built.

SCARLETT

As the months pass, the house begins to feel more like a shared home. The rooms, once filled only with Eli and Lily's memories, now echo with the sounds of our combined lives—our laughter mingling with the playful chaos that comes with preparing for a new baby. Days blur into each other in a rhythm of doctor's appointments, baby shopping, and nursery decorating, each moment weaving us closer together. I add little rituals of my own—Sunday pancakes, candles lit even on weeknights—tiny touches that make the space ours.

Every time I catch Eli's eye—whether he's painting the nursery walls or carefully assembling the crib—I feel my love deepen, anchoring me in this life we're building.

One morning, we're in a baby store surrounded by rows of impossibly small clothes and strollers engineered like small aircraft. Eli lifts a neutral onesie, its size absurd in his hands. "What do you think?" he asks.

"It's perfect," I whisper, pressing a hand to my belly. Awe climbs fast, tightening my throat.

Lily darts over, hugging a teddy bear to her chest. "I'm going to be the best big sister ever!" she declares.

"You already are," I tell her, meaning every word. Eli's eyes meet mine, sure and certain, like he feels it too.

Not that everything is seamless. Blending our lives comes with its bumps. The fridge, for one. His shelves are columns by height; my oat creamer breaks rank. Or the morning the dishes piled too high, or the night clutter outran my tidying. Little sparks that don't break us but remind me our defaults aren't the same.

But we find our footing. He resets the house at night, lining things back into order. I leave Lily's crooked drawings taped where she put them, even when they overlap the light switch. Some days it leans his way, some days mine, but together it starts to feel like home. Being folded into their rituals feels like being carried forward—like belonging without effort.

One night, after a long stretch of nursery prep, I curl against him on the couch, exhausted but content. "This isn't always easy," I admit. "But it's worth it. Every part of it."

His arm tightens around me, lips brushing my hair. "I know. I wouldn't trade it either."

The summer air drifts through the open window. Our baby kicks beneath my hand. The word home settles into place—not borrowed, not temporary, but real.

CHAPTER 29

Storm & Steering

Contractions hit. He keeps you breathing.

SCARLETT

The first cramp slices me awake, sharp enough to wrench me off the mattress. My stomach hollows, cold rushing under my ribs, breath snagging halfway down. My hand clamps around Eli's wrist before words can form.

"Eli," I gasp, throat pinched. "It's time."

For a blink his eyes flare wide—raw panic, unhidden. Then his face resets, calm and focused, as if a switch has flipped. Jeans already in his grip, bag already in his hand, like he's been running this drill in his head for weeks.

Another contraction claws through me. I double over, one palm braced to the wall, the nightstand knob digging into my other hand like an anchor. Eli's arm is around me before I sway, his voice low and even. "Breathe with me, Scarlett. In... out. Again." His thumb strokes the back of my hand, steady as a metronome.

From the hallway: a creak, soft footsteps. "Daddy?"

Lily stands in the doorway, hair tangled, her nightgown twisted at the hem, bunny clutched tight. Sleep still clings to her eyes, but fear pinches her face.

Eli crouches, keeping one arm around me. "Sweetheart, the baby's ready to come. Uncle Mark's on his way. You'll stay with Aunt Sam tonight." His tone doesn't waver—gentle but sure, like a handrail in the dark.

Her lip trembles. "Now?"

I crouch as far as my body allows, sweat slick on my temple, voice ragged. "She's going to need her big sister—and she's got the perfect one."

Eli scoops her close, holding her for one fierce heartbeat. His voice catches even as he steadies it. "We love you. It won't be long before you meet her."

Headlights wash across the windows, tires crunching to a stop outside. A door slams, and then Mark's voice carries up the walk—low, steady, unhurried. Safe. Seconds later, he fills the doorway, reaching for Lily's hand. Relief floods me through the pain. She isn't alone. She won't be.

Outside, the air slams heavy—summer heat mixed with the metallic tang of an oncoming storm. Cicadas shrill in the trees; the pavement still radiates the day's warmth. Another contraction folds me forward, but Eli's hand never loosens, steering me into the car.

Inside, the leather seats cling hot against my skin. Eli cracks the windows, lets the damp night air roll over me. I focus on the rhythm of whoosh, whoosh as the dark streets slip past, each streetlamp blurring into the next.

At the hospital doors, the blast of AC shocks goose-bumps across my arms. The antiseptic bite of the waiting room cuts against the storm-damp air still clinging to my skin. A nurse presses ice water into my palm; condensation runs cold down my wrist as Eli handles the words I can't. Insurance, forms, answers.

Hours dissolve into contractions, the storm finally breaking outside. Rain lashes against wide windows, thunder rolling low, lightning etching Eli's profile where he kneels by the bed. His hand never leaves mine. "You're doing amazing," he whispers, voice steady as stone. "I'm proud of you."

Those words hold me up when my body feels like it's tearing apart. Machines beep, nurses move in practiced rhythm, but all I see are his eyes pulling me through.

And then—the cry. Thin, unsteady, perfect. Relief breaks me open.

Eli's tears shine as he holds her, his shirt damp with sweat and storm. He presses her tiny body against me, his hand still steadying me. "She's perfect," he whispers, voice raw.

Her fingers curl around mine, impossibly small. The name rises, clear and certain, in both of us at once.

"Delilah," we breathe together. A memory from that first night—the throwback song, the spark that pulled us close. It fits like it was always hers.

I nod through tears. "Perfect. Just like her."

Lightning flashes beyond the glass, thunder fading soft and far. The storm eases, but inside this room, everything begins.

CHAPTER 30
Dawn & Delilah

One cry. The axis tilts forever.

ELI

The world shifted the moment she cried. Every axis tilted.

Delilah. Our Delilah.

Scarlett's asleep now, body wrung out and still, her hair damp against the pillow. The fluorescent light washes her pale, but there's a serenity in her face I've never seen—hard-earned, luminous. She looks fragile—skin pale, body spent—and unstoppable, strength carved into every line of her face.

I glance down at the bundle in my arms. She's impossibly small—seven pounds, nineteen inches, a universe contained in cloth. Her fist curls tight around my pinky, grip strong for something so new. She sighs, little lungs testing air, and the sound cuts me to the bone.

I catalog details the way my mind always does: the fuzz of dark hair damp on her head, the squeak she makes when she shifts, the steady rise of her chest. I log each one like data points, but they don't stay clinical. They shift into awe.

Scarlett stirs once, lashes fluttering. Her voice is shredded from the hours behind her, but she whispers, "She's just right."

I bend, brush her hair back. "So are you." Her eyes close again, but her fingers twitch toward mine, like she can't rest without contact. I lace them together. Even wrung out from labor, she's arresting. Desire hums low—not sharp, but a steady thrum braided with awe.

The nurse slips in, checks vitals, murmurs encouragement. I nod, but I don't hand Delilah over. My arms won't release her.

The storm outside has spent itself. Dawn glows faint through storm-washed glass. Inside, it's just us—three heartbeats tethered.

When Scarlett settles deeper, I finally pull out my phone. Morning. Time to call.

Sam first. She answers groggy, but awake instantly when she hears my voice. Lily's on the line seconds later, small and breathless.

"Daddy?"

"You've got a baby sister," I tell her, and my throat locks when I hear her little gasp.

"Really? Right now?"

"Right now. She's perfect, bug. You'll meet her later today."

I just know I'll be the best big sister," she whispers, certain. Like it's already written.

"You already are."

After Lily, the rest. Dad and Patricia—voices breaking with joy, already promising they're on their way. Mark, swearing he and Sam will be at the hospital before lunch. Tessa, crying so hard she can barely get the words out, vowing she's bringing balloons whether we want them or not.

The silence afterward is heavy, but not empty. I stand at the window with Delilah against my chest, her warmth bleeding through the pink hospital blanket. She shifts, sighs, curls closer, like I'm her world already.

I've built systems, mapped contingencies, solved problems down to their smallest part. But this—this tiny life pressed against me—is different. Not a system I built. A family we created. And it feels exactly right.

I lay Delilah in the bassinet, brush a finger across her cheek, then sit back to watch Scarlett breathe, steady and alive.

Nothing I've ever built matters more than this—Scarlett, Lily, Delilah. Us.

CHAPTER 31
Rockers & Roots

She calls you Mommy. It fits like truth.

SCARLETT

Days collapse into nights, nights fold back into days. Time isn't linear anymore; it's measured in feedings, diaper changes, the soft sigh of Delilah's breath against my skin.

My body aches in ways I couldn't have imagined—heavy breasts, muscles sore from new rhythms, eyes burning from sleepless hours. But every time she latches, her tiny hand resting against me, the pain softens under the weight of awe. She knows me already. My heartbeat, my smell, my voice. It undoes me.

Lily is radiant in her new role. She fetches diapers, pats Delilah's back with surprising gentleness, curls up beside me to read in a whisper while I nurse. She chatters about how she'll teach her sister to color inside the lines, how she'll share her stuffed bunny but only "for emergencies." Her pride glows so brightly it feels like the walls themselves hold the warmth.

But sometimes, when the house quiets, I catch something else in her eyes. A wrinkle between her brows when she stands in the doorway watching me rock Delilah. The way she holds her favorite stuffed animal tighter than usual.

One afternoon, I find her curled on her bed, bunny clutched to her chest, lips pressed tight. I sit beside her, smoothing her hair back. "Hey, sweetheart. What's wrong?"

She hesitates, then blurts, "Is Delilah going to take you away?"

The words lance straight through me. I gather her into my arms, holding her small body close. "Never, Lily. Not ever. You're just as important as Delilah. I love you both, the same, forever."

She buries her face against my neck. "I love you too, Mommy."

The word lands like a lightning strike—sudden, searing, reshaping everything in its path. Mommy. She hasn't said that name since Thanksgiving. In my head, I still hear her little voice: *Are you gonna be my Mommy?* I never pushed, never let myself expect it. And now here it is, hers to give. It feels like belonging made real.

Eli appears in the doorway, quiet, watching. His expression wrecks me—lips pressed, eyes shining, like he's waited his whole life for this.

"Everything okay?" he asks softly.

I nod, still holding Lily. "More than okay."

Lily leans back to beam up at him. "Mommy said I'm just as important as Delilah."

Eli's breath catches; his eyes meet mine over her head. Gratitude. Love. Relief. All unguarded, written plain.

He crosses the room and folds us both into his arms. His chest is warm against my back, his voice steady in my ear. "She's right. We're one big family. And we love you so much."

The house exhales with us—Delilah's faint coos, the cicadas outside, the hum of the fan through the open window. For the first time since bringing her home, the chaos feels quiet. Whole.

Later that night, after Delilah is settled again, Eli and I sit in the nursery with the nightlight casting golden shadows across the room. His arms circle me, my head pressed to his chest, the quiet, even thump of his heart grounding me.

"This is where I'm meant to be," I whisper. "With you. With Lily. With Delilah. With all of us."

His lips brush the top of my head. "This is everything I ever wanted." The kiss lingers, and beneath the steadiness I catch the pull that's always there—heat waiting under the tenderness. It steadies me, knowing the fire hasn't dimmed. It's just folded into the quiet, waiting for space.

The rhythm of the rocker lulls us, the night pressing close around the windows. Exhausting, imperfect, beautiful—that's what this is.

And for the first time in my life, I don't just feel like I belong. I know it.

Epilogue: Masks & Forever

Full circle. No more goodbyes.

ELI

The house hums with Halloween—laughter, Lily's squeals darting through the living room. Pumpkins grin from every corner, faux cobwebs dangle in the doorways, paper ghosts sway in the draft from the cracked window. The scent of pumpkin cookies mingles with crisp autumn air, grounding the room in cozy familiarity.

Lily, my little witch, shows off her broomstick to anyone who'll look, her floppy hat sliding over her eyes every few minutes. Scarlett crouches by the couch, fixing the tiny black cat ears on Delilah's head, her smile soft and fierce at once. Our baby's first Halloween—Scarlett's little kitten, matching her mama's modest black cat costume this year.

It makes me smile, remembering last Halloween: Scarlett in that Catwoman costume that haunted me for weeks. Tonight's outfit is toned down, but the sweetness of her matching with Delilah feels more intimate—mother and daughter claiming their place together. With Lily as a witch, Scarlett as the mama cat, and Delilah as the kitten, they're perfectly coordinated. A family.

I glance down at my own T-shirt—"I'm Just Here for the Candy"—and Scarlett immediately narrows her eyes in mock disapproval.

"Seriously? No Zorro costume this year? I was looking forward to that."

I shrug. "Deal was Catwoman and Zorro. You broke it—so boring dad it is."

She shakes her head, laughing. "You're never boring, Eli. But still... I wanted to see Zorro."

The doorbell rings. Samantha and Mark burst in with their boys—one a roaring dinosaur, the other a wild-haired mad scientist. Chaos explodes as costumes are compared and candy buckets waved. Mark smirks at my T-shirt. "Classic move—hide in plain sight as a dad joke."

"Stealth mode works. Nobody suspects the dad joke."

Samantha cuddles Delilah, promising Scarlett she'll be fine overnight. Scarlett hesitates, but trusts her. We huddle for a quick video call with Dad and Patricia—Frankenstein's monster and his bride—delighted by the chaos. A year ago, everything felt impossible—complications, secrets. But their steady support helped turn it into this: a messy, remarkable love story that everyone accepts.

The kids spill outside for trick-or-treating, Lily skipping between Scarlett and me, Delilah gurgling in my arms. The streets glow with orange lights, laughter, the crunch of leaves. Looking at them—my girls—I feel it in my chest. A year ago, I was searching. Tonight, I'm home.

Back at the house, once Sam and Mark load their boys and Lily into the van for another neighborhood run, I turn to Scarlett. Her nerves linger, but so does her curiosity—she knows I've got something planned.

I kiss her, long and deep, then whisper, "Wait here. No peeking."

In the bedroom, I tug on the cape, fasten the mask, adjust the hat. My pulse hammers but steadies the second I picture her face.

"Close your eyes," I call. When she opens them, her smile lights brighter than the jack-o'-lanterns. "You're wearing it!" she squeals, rushing into my arms.

I drop to one knee, box hidden under the cape. "Last Halloween you walked in as Catwoman and wrecked my system. Tonight, I'm asking you to wreck every plan I make from here on out—on purpose. Marry me."

Her tears spill as fast as her "Yes!" She throws herself into my arms. The kiss blazes—no restraint, no calculation—proof that even after sleepless nights and chaos, the fire between us is intact. Certain. Ours.

We tumble back into the bedroom, laughter and heat wrapping around us, but this time there's no uncertainty, no goodbye waiting in the morning. Just love, promise, and forever.

Sometime after the laughter fades into whispers and sleep, I murmur against her hair: "Tomorrow—pancakes."

And at dawn, I keep it. Batter and coffee thick in the air as I balance the tray into the room—pancakes, berries, eggs, steam curling at the edges. Scarlett's eyes widen as I set it down. "You actually did it," she teases, but her gaze lingers on the ring. "Feels like a dream."

"It's real," I assure her. "And it's just the beginning."

By the time the tray is finished, flour dusts the counter, batter streaks my shirt, coffee drips where I misjudged the filter. Normally I'd hate the mess. Today, I don't care. Scarlett's smile when she sees it all is worth more than any perfectly clean kitchen.

Minutes later, the front door bursts open—Sam, Mark, Lily, and a sleepy Delilah back from their night. Scarlett gathers Delilah, relief flooding her features. Lily climbs into bed, bubbling: "Delilah was so good last night!"

Scarlett kisses her hair, whispering back, "Thank you, sweetheart."

I pull them all close—Scarlett, Lily, Delilah—the breakfast tray wobbling as we laugh together.

This is my forever. Not just Halloween night. Not just one year. Every dawn, every bedtime story, every pumpkin cookie cooling on the counter. Our family. Our home. Our story still being written.

I thought order was what made me steady. Turns out it was them all along.

Think you've seen it all? Not even close. Scarlett's POV is hotter, dirtier, and dripping with the spice you've been waiting for.

Read Scarlett's Bonus Epilogue

→ https://BookHip.com/BMSWZBL

(Scan the QR to open.)

About the Author

Kandie Kissimmie writes cozy-and-spicy romances with protective heroes, creative-at-heart heroines, and guaranteed HEAs—often featuring age gap, single dads, best friend's dad/dad's best friend, and deliciously tense proximity.

A Midwestern former teacher, she's a homebody who loves fall, long walks, and food-sensitivity-friendly baking. She lives with her family (and one opinionated cat).

Find 40+ stories on Ream, with select titles on KU, plus bonus scenes and updates:

kandiekissimmie.com
reamstories.com/kandiekissimmie

Printed in Dunstable, United Kingdom